Kristin felt as though she were on the brink of triggering an avalanche.

Although the sunny meadow was warm and bursting with more wildflowers than snow, Kristin still held her breath as if she were skiing over an icy crest that was about to give way as Gray slowly rolled toward her and she slid her hand up his shoulders and down the column of his back. His muscles quivered under her touch, as if coming fully awake after a long slumber.

"This is insane," he groaned. He pressed her back against the heat of the mountain, sandwiching her between it and the warmth pouring from his chest. Her lids drooped; she was drugged by the heady fragrance of the wildflowers and Gray's own male smell. She threaded her fingers through his sun-streaked hair and brought his head down. The avalanche had begun to fall.

Kristin could feel the thunder of his heartbeat resonating in her chest to match the racing beat of her own heart. He parted her lips, his tongue hungrily exploring hers. His hand lingered over the dip of her waist, the arch of her rib cage, the thrust of her breasts.

Kristin gasped with pleasure. She gazed at the man who had excited her with such force. Feeling her scrutiny, he opened his eyes. He had the dazed appearance of a man fighting his way out of a coma. Then his eyes narrowed and grew cold, dissipating the warmth they had shared.

"I'm sorry," he said. "I took advantage of my position."

Also by Tory Cates

A High, Hard Land

Different Dreams

Cloud Waltzer

Handful of Sky

Where Aspens Quake

Tory Cates

Pocket Books
New York London Toronto Sydney New Delhi

Pocket Books
A Division of Simon & Schuster, Inc.
1230 Avenue of the Americas
New York, NY 10020

Previously published in 1983 by Silhouette Books

First Pocket Books paperback edition April 2014

Designed by Lewelin Polanco
Cover illustration by Craig White

Manufactured in the United States of America

10 9 8 7 6 5 4 3 2 1

ISBN 978-1-4767-3257-2
ISBN 978-1-4767-3262-6 (ebook)

Hi, George!

Where Aspens Quake

Chapter 1

K*ristin turned off the ignition* of her battered old Volvo station wagon and slumped down behind the steering wheel. Just getting this far, the parking lot of Albuquerque's Old Town, had required a major effort of will, and the determination she had managed to generate was beginning to flag. With a sigh she hoisted herself out of the car.

She unfolded her five-foot, eleven-inch frame and stood up tall, or, to use a word her mother preferred to describe her height, *statuesque*, and erect. The slump was a posture Kristin found neither comfortable nor natural. Unlike a lot of tall women, she'd never been ashamed of her height and had never slouched to minimize it. She inhaled deeply and New Mexico's air, alive with the magic of late autumn, worked a minor spell on her. A touch of the bouncy enthusiasm that was characteristic of her returned and, for the first time in two weeks, there was a spring, however slight, to her step as she ventured toward the plaza.

Once the heart of a frontier city, Albuquerque's Old Town plaza now served as the focal point for arts-and-crafts fairs and fiestas and as a shady respite for weary tourists. The summer visitors had long since departed. Aside from a few withered cottonwood leaves rattling between the white wrought-iron benches and the bandstand, the plaza was deserted.

Kristin glanced desultorily into the windows of the shops ringing the plaza. Displays of sand paintings, postcards, and desert perfumes were so familiar that they made no more of an impression upon her than did the sight of Native American vendors, wrapped beneath woolly Pendleton blankets, their jewelry and other wares spread at their feet. A gust of wind funneled down the long portal running the length of the shops and swirled up her skirt. She grabbed at the billowing material and twisted around to hold it down. She ended up facing herself straight on in a shop window and at the sight came as close to laughing as she had in two weeks. Wearing a full denim prairie skirt, riding boots, a ruffled blouse with a black string tie at the throat, and a lined vest, she realized she looked like a cross between Annie Oakley and Annie Hall.

She sighed. *So much for the old image.* Not that it mattered now anyway.

Her mood of amused resignation held up halfway across the plaza, then abruptly dissolved as she confronted the Church of San Felipe de Neri. It was as magnificent as ever, its twin spires cutting patterns of stark white against a sky of such an achingly pure, deep blue that for a moment it made her yearn for the ability to dive *up* and swim through it. At least that was how its beauty had always affected Kristin. And that was what she had tried to convey in her photographs of the church, founded in 1706 in a hostile land by Franciscan fathers with dreams of spreading their cherished faith to a new world. The memory that her own, far more mundane, dream had shattered and that she was on her way now to pick up the pieces overran her like the fast-moving shadow of a hawk closing in on a baby chick. She crumpled onto a wrought-iron bench.

How much more of this can I take? she asked herself. Because it wasn't just the church, it was a hundred and one spots in and around Albuquerque that were precious to her and that she'd tried to interpret on film. For the past two weeks, ever since Felicia Cliver's review had appeared, she'd felt as if she were living in a minefield. Everywhere she turned, cruel reminders of the folly of her ambition waited to explode in her face and rip open the hurt once again.

The wind, which had seemed brisk and refreshing a moment before, now tore at her with a forlorn chill.

Whether it was the wind or grief for a stillborn dream that brought stinging tears to her eyes, Kristin didn't know or care. Tendrils of auburn hair escaped from the thick braid down her back and whipped at her face. As if by instinct, her gaze searched out and found the Sandia Mountains that cradled Albuquerque within their rocky grasp. They beckoned to Kristin, promising the comfort and escape she had always found skiing along a mountain trail. Never had she needed the peace and tranquility of a secluded, snow-frosted cross-country ski trail more than she did at that moment.

The tower bells tolled the noon hour. Kristin had taken an early lunch so that she could dash over to the gallery before the owner, Alana Moorington, made her daily afternoon appearance. The thought of a chance meeting with Alana spurred Kristin back into reluctant motion.

The gallery was set among a trendy cluster of shops on one of the roads that spoked off of the plaza. The last time she had been there was opening night. Where it once had been the object of her most intense professional longings—the best photography gallery in the city—she now approached it with something close to dread. The sign reading APERTURE GALLERY swung above the door in the early-November wind and was reflected in the gallery's sidewalk-to-ceiling windows. Kristin could see Tracy, the gallery manager, directing the chaos that accompanied the hanging of a new show. Kristin recognized the color prints. They had been taken by a professor she had studied under at the university. She hoped sincerely that he would fare better than she had.

A bell tinkled as she pushed open the heavy wooden door carved with a camera-shutter design that resembled a blossoming flower. The gallery floor was covered with charcoal-gray industrial carpeting. The walls were a light oyster-gray, the color having been carefully chosen to enhance Kristin's black-and-white exhibit. Now that a color show was replacing it, the walls were reverting to their original basic white. Track lights ran across the ceiling waiting to be refocused on the latest additions.

"Kristin, there you are," Tracy called out. The gallery manager, a chubby young woman in paint-spattered jeans, left her two helpers whitewashing the walls. She started to hug Kristin, then pulled back with a laugh.

"I don't imagine that white polka dots would do much for your outfit."

Kristin faked what she hoped would pass for a hearty laugh. "Well, here I am. I've returned to the scene of the crime to pick up my 'postcard renditions of life in a tourist's landscape.'" Kristin quoted the words from Felicia Cliver's review with ease. They had been seared into her memory that awful morning following the opening of her one-woman show when she'd read them online before the paper was even printed. Tracy noticed the slight catch in her voice and the red-rimmed eyes that contradicted Kristin's artificial smile.

"Come on into the back," Tracy said, taking Kristin by the arm. "I'll scrounge us up a cup of tea."

"No, Trace," Kristin tried to refuse. "You've got an opening tonight. I know you have a zillion things to do."

"And I've been doing them and I need a break. This very instant to be precise."

Kristin breathed in the orange-scented steam of the hot tea and remembered the frantic exhilaration of her own opening as she and Tracy had rushed to finish mounting all her photographs, then debated exactly where each one should be hung.

"Kristin." Tracy's voice was low and comforting. "I know this is probably silly advice and impossible to follow to boot, but don't take it so hard."

Kristin didn't have to ask what "it" was. For the past two weeks, she'd been brooding over the scathing review of the first full-fledged exhibition of her photographs. Then, to compound the injury, Tracy had called her the day before to ask if she could come by and pick up her prints; Alana had booked in another show and was cutting hers short by a full two weeks.

"It's good advice, Tracy," Kristin agreed. "And I'm trying like the devil to follow it. Not to let this get me down any more than it already has. But it's been hard, real hard." Kristin hastily looked down into her mug as she felt the sting in her eyes that presaged the spill of tears. It was a feeling that had grown tediously familiar.

"Hey, it's okay." Tracy put a hand on Kristin's shoulder.

Kristin attempted a feeble laugh. "This is ridiculous. I haven't opened up the waterworks the way I've been doing for the past two weeks since my science fair project in junior high lost in the regional finals." Kristin glanced up, a self-deprecating smile quivering on her lips. Serious again, she admitted, "I suppose it's because I wanted this show to succeed so badly."

"I feel partially responsible for everything," Tracy said ruefully. "For how it all turned out."

"Oh, Trace, why? Because you 'discovered' me? Talked Alana into giving me my own show? How were you to know I'd bomb?" Kristin congratulated herself for being able to utter that last word without any hint of puddling up.

"Kristin, you didn't bomb," Tracy demurred forcefully. "One, I repeat, one, lone critic didn't like the show, and for God only knows what reasons."

"Let me give you a few she supplied herself," Kristin offered. "And I quote, 'Kristin Jonsson's gauzy landscapes and saccharine-sweet still lifes left this reviewer with a cloying aftertaste.'"

"She *was* pretty brutal," Tracy said softly, as if she could somehow buffer the harsh words with her gentle tone. "But that just proves that she didn't really see what was in your photographs. She missed entirely what you were saying."

"It wasn't just her, Trace. Not one of my photos sold. The public agreed with the review. Alana had to close the show early or you would have gone bankrupt."

"This gallery isn't run to make money, you know that."

Kristin was familiar with the real reasons behind the Aperture Gallery's existence. First and foremost it was a tax write-off for Geoffrey Moorington, Alana's husband. For Alana it was a way to one-up her friends. Owning a photo gallery had so much more cachet than modeling in Junior League charity fashion shows or being a docent at the Albuquerque Museum.

"Besides," Tracy continued, "people are afraid to take a chance with any new artist until he or she is officially sanctioned."

"And I obviously did not get the official sanction."

"Kristin, I know that we haven't been friends long, but I feel close to you. I suppose because you put so much of yourself into your work and it appealed to me the first time you brought your portfolio in. And it still does." Tracy stopped and stared at Kristin to emphasize her sincerity.

Kristin was warmed and comforted by her support.

"Anyway, you're taking this all a lot harder than I would have expected you to."

Kristin was surprised at Tracy's perceptiveness. She, Kristin, had always been noted for her bubbly optimism and resilience. Even in graduate school when she had received a blistering critique of her early work, she'd believed so strongly in what she was doing and in her own personal vision that she'd bounced right back, never deviating from the individual course she'd plotted for herself. But this, she reminded herself grimly, was the real world; this was where critiques started to matter, to direct the course of lives. She wasn't frolicking in the sheltered groves of academe any longer.

"You're right," Kristin admitted. "I suppose I pinned too many hopes on this one show. But it's what I've been working toward for years. I mean, I left everything—my friends, my family—when I came out here from Wisconsin to study photography, to be a 'real' photographer. Then, for the last two years since graduation, I've been doing hackwork during the day to make enough to buy materials to do my own work in my spare time and keep clinging to the illusion that I was a 'real' photographer. It just all came crashing down in one night."

"Kristin, you're talking like you've gone blind," Tracy said with a touch of sternness. "Why are you any less of a photographer now than you were two weeks ago?"

"I know what you're trying to do, Tracy, and I appreciate it. I really do. Intellectually I even agree with you. I've given myself a dozen pep talks and said just the same thing. And they work too, for a while, at least until I drive by that wall of graffiti on Central or see the neon signs at sunset compressed against the mountains or any of the other things I photographed. Then all the pep talks dissolve into this great big blobby, weepy feeling inside that I just haven't been able to shake."

Tracy nodded her head as if she finally understood the depth of Kristin's distress. "Have you thought about leaving Albuquerque for a while?"

"Every day," Kristin replied without hesitation. "Especially when I go to work and find out that I'm going to be creating bar graphs or photographing some new pressure valve all day. A slight hitch always comes up, though, whenever I consider any escape plan: My bank account stays perpetually in the slim two-figure category."

"That probably won't get you to the Bahamas."

"Probably not." The two women laughed conspiratorially. Kristin felt buoyed up, renewed, by the tea and Tracy's good-natured banter.

"Don't you have any friends you could stay with for a while?" Tracy picked up the thread of her inquiry again. "Any relatives you could stand for a short vacation?"

"I don't think it would be a question of my being able to stand them," Kristin countered. "I've been so dreary lately that I'm tired of being around myself. No, I really don't think I'd make a terrifically charming houseguest."

She paused and an image surfaced in her mind, an image of a mountain, any mountain, beckoning with its promise of an icy-blue refuge. "You know what I'd really like?" Kristin began wistfully, knowing full well that she was only giving voice to yet another impossible dream. "To spend some time up in the mountains. Away from Albuquerque, away from everyone I know." She dismissed the thought with a curt laugh as soon as she'd uttered it.

"But that would be the perfect solution," Tracy protested.

"Perfect, except for the small matter of being able to feed and shelter myself," Kristin reminded her.

"Aren't there jobs at the ski areas? You do ski, don't you?"

"Cross-country," Kristin said. "That's a completely different sport from downhill, which is just about all they do up in the Sandias."

"There are other mountains in New Mexico. What about the Sangre de Cristos up north?"

"I've been up there hiking in the summer, but I've never done any skiing in that area. I have no idea how popular cross-country skiing is up there."

"There's a real easy way to find out," Tracy said, turning away to dig through a pile of books and magazines heaped beside the table where she kept track of the gallery's bookkeeping.

Kristin wanted to tell Tracy not to waste any more of her time with the silly notion, but it had obviously caught her fancy.

"Here it is." Tracy enthusiastically dug out the latest copy of *Around New Mexico*, a guide to the state's recreational facilities. "Let's see, cross-country skiing, cross-country skiing," she muttered, running a finger down the index. She flipped back through the pages and announced triumphantly, "Here you are, CROSS-COUNTRY SKIING, AREAS AND LODGES, SANGRE DE CRISTOS: THE TAOS HIGH COUNTRY LODGE, OWNER, GRAYSON LOWREY. Grayson Lowrey," she mused. "I've heard that name before. Oh, right, now I remember. He owns Powderhorn Ski Valley and a couple of other smaller downhill resorts in the southern part of the state. Anyway," Tracy said, returning to the business at hand, "what do you think?"

"About what?"

"About trying to find a job there. How long have you been cross-country skiing?"

"Gosh." Kristin stammered as she mentally calculated the years. "Fifteen years, at least. I started in Wisconsin back in the days when the only people doing that kind of skiing were scoutmasters and Scandinavian immigrants who grew up cross-countrying back in Sweden and Norway. My father just happened to be both."

"Great," Tracy burst out as if the matter were decided, "you can instruct at this High Country Lodge."

Kristin was dumbfounded. The last thing she'd anticipated when she'd walked in a few minutes before was to be considering a retreat to the Sangre de Cristos. Oddly enough, though, she couldn't think of one solid objection to raise to Tracy's unexpected suggestion. Certainly not her job; that was one of the chief contributors to her depression. And her relationship with Dennis Hascomb? For some time now she'd felt uneasy about it. There wasn't anything she could specifically put her finger on. Dennis was invariably amusing and certainly generous when they went out. But there was something vaguely unsubstantial about what they shared—like a lovely, shiny sheet of thin ice that couldn't bear any weight. It was an unsettling feeling that had grown worse over the past two critical weeks when Kristin had mostly wanted someone sturdy to lean on.

"Like I said, it would be the perfect solution." Tracy continued to expand on her "perfect solution." "You'd be away from Albuquerque, in a completely new environment. You wouldn't be imposing on anyone. I can tell from your work that you love the outdoors. It would give you a chance to lick your wounds, recharge artistically, and come back with some new stuff that will knock Cliver's socks off."

Kristin felt like hugging Tracy, for her support went far beyond the polite words of encouragement her friends had been murmuring to her, friends like Dennis

Hascomb. The difference was that Tracy clearly believed what she was saying. She really thought that Kristin *could* come back and knock Felicia Cliver's Dior pantyhose off.

Kristin was trying to frame the words to express her appreciation when Tracy glanced at her watch. "Oh Lord, look at the time. Alana will be here any minute and I haven't finished half of what I should have done by now. And you had better get back to work yourself. You don't want to lose the job you already have before you've even decided if you're ready for a new one."

"How right you are," Kristin agreed. "The head of the graphics department is a bureaucrat to the core. He thinks if he lets any of the bohemian artist types that work for him get away with *anything*, even being five minutes late from lunch, we'll all just kick over the traces and start using nude models in his electronics catalogs or Day-Glo paints on the sales charts."

Smiling, Tracy led the way to a back room where Kristin's photographs were neatly stacked in upright bins. "If you'd like," she volunteered, "I can get one of the guys to haul these out to your car for you."

"No, thanks." Kristin refused the generous offer. It was rare that anyone ever assumed that someone of her height could use a helping hand, particularly when that person was as overburdened as Tracy was at the moment. "You need all your manpower now. I've kept you long enough. Just unlock the back door and I'll pull around. It'll be a cinch then to load them up."

"Deal," Tracy agreed, unlocking the door. "I'd better get back out there before they decide to whitewash Professor Collins's prints. I'll call you later this afternoon."

"Thanks," Kristin said, holding Tracy's eyes with her own gray-streaked green ones. "Thanks for everything."

Tracy flapped a hand at her, dismissing Kristin's gratitude. Kristin hurried back across the plaza to her car and brought it around to the gallery's alley entrance. Though she tried to take Tracy's advice and not dwell on her failure, the inevitable glimpses that Kristin caught of her photographs started a complicated brew of emotions percolating through her.

As she carefully transferred to the blanket-covered back of her station wagon the first batch of the sixteen-by-eleven-inch gelatin silver prints that she had so meticulously created from actual black-and-white film that she'd developed herself, she felt like a mother who's been called in because her child has been acting up at school. The prints *were* her children and, according to at least one authority figure, they'd behaved badly. On that score they had publicly humiliated her. But on a deeper level, a level that even Kristin herself was not yet fully aware of, she still believed more in her artistic offspring than in the opinion of the authority figure. Like the loyal mother, in her heart of hearts she stood behind her children. Kristin was taking out the second load when the studiedly cultured voice reached her ears.

"Oh, Andrew, these are simply exquisite." It was Alana Moorington. Kristin guessed that "Andrew" must be Professor Andrew Collins, whose work was being put on display.

"Your use of negative form is absolutely inspired," Alana raved on.

If the sound of Alana's voice hadn't depressed her so much, Kristin might have laughed. "Use of negative form" indeed; that was precisely what the gallery owner had said to her after Tracy had brought her work to Alana's attention and recommended that Kristin be given her own show. The lavish shower of praise had abruptly dried up, though, when Felicia Cliver publicly disagreed with the opinion that Kristin Jonsson had a shred of talent. What an embarrassment that must have been for Alana, Kristin thought, with something approaching glee. Here the poor woman had devoted her life to being a trendsetter, then was found guilty in print of harboring such a master of the gauche as herself.

"And back here is storage space where you can . . ." Alana breezed into the back room with Professor Collins under her chicly tailored wing. "Uh, why, hello . . ."

"Kristin." Kristin supplied her name rather than allow Alana to fumble any further for it, even though it had been just a few weeks since she was the one being given the owner-guided tour of the Aperture Gallery. "Hello, Professor Collins." Kristin smiled pleasantly at her former instructor.

The short, bespectacled art professor nodded a greeting at her with the same sort of awkwardness people display around someone who's just had a death in the family.

Of course, Kristin thought, *he thinks my career, or any hope I had of a "real" art career, died with Felicia Cliver's venomous review.* "I was just clearing out here," Kristin said in a statement of the obvious. Hurriedly, she gathered up her few remaining prints.

"Good luck with your show, Professor Collins," she said, pausing beside the door.

"Oh, yeah, sure, thanks," came the stammered reply. Alana stood beside him, a haute couture fashion model's haughty smile frozen on her lips.

The worst is over. Kristin forced herself to keep repeating that thought as she drove back to her office. *The worst is over.* She chanted the words like an incantation to ward off the tears building once again behind her eyes. She was sick of weeping, sick of humiliation. She was not a weeper or a groveler and neither Felicia Cliver nor Alana Moorington would reduce her to either. The healthy glow of anger dried her tears. Unfortunately, the route back to her office took her past several of the scenes she'd tried to interpret on film.

It's just not fair, Kristin thought. Every time she started to reconstruct her defenses, the city launched a sneak attack on her. She wondered if recovering from a love affair was this painful and assumed that the feeling a spurned lover had when she saw all the places where she'd gone with her ex was probably similar. She assumed but couldn't really say because, while her tall, titian-haired good looks had always assured her of ample male company, no one man had ever emerged as a serious threat to her first love: her art.

Mr. Pershing looked pointedly at his watch as Kristin entered the office with GRAPHIC ARTS DIVISION stenciled on the door. She was five minutes late. Her supervisor gave her a sour look as she headed to her cubicle at the back of the long, open room. The Graphic Arts Division was part of a large electronics firm and, when she'd first started work two years before, each artist had had his or her own office with a door that actually shut. When Mr. Pershing took over a few months later, however, he'd had all the partitions ripped out and a warren of doorless cubicles installed so that he could keep an eye on his staff at all times.

Knowing that Mr. Pershing's eyes and scowl were following her back to her cubicle, Kristin quickly put away her purse and sat down behind her oversized monitor to continue working on a map of all the electronics firm's retail outlets. A technical illustrator had quit two months before and never been replaced; instead, her workload had simply been added to Kristin's. She added several southwestern states and dotted them with the silver stars that represented retail outlets.

While her well-practiced hands moved and clicked the mouse fluidly to produce a neat, attractive bit of graphic art, her mind whirled over other thoughts. She reflected on the irony of a person like herself training for years to develop a talent for self-expression, then ending up putting stars on charts to be used by some vice president she would never meet for a sales presentation she would never hear. The phone beside her computer buzzed. The company operator informed her that she had a call on line five. Kristin cradled the receiver between her ear and shoulder so that she could still work as she talked, then pushed the appropriate button on her phone.

"How'd it go at Aperture?" It was Dennis Hascomb, the man Kristin had been dating for nearly a year.

"It wasn't an experience I'd like to relive every day," she answered, keeping her voice low so that the artist on the other side of the plastic partition couldn't overhear her conversation, "but I managed to retrieve my prints."

"Did you run into Alana?"

"Yes."

Dennis was just starting out in the law firm owned by Geoffrey Moorington and he thrived on any details about his boss's wife. Listening to the eagerness in his voice, it suddenly struck Kristin that Dennis had generally thrived on *all* the details of her failed exhibit.

"Well, thank God, it's all over, right?" he asked, seeking her confirmation.

"The exhibit is most definitely down," Kristin answered, slightly put off by Dennis's enthusiasm.

"Now, maybe we can start seeing each other like normal people."

"Were we so *abnormal* before?" Kristin queried.

"You know what I mean, Kris. You were so caught up in this photography thing that you were either in the darkroom or down on Central stopping traffic so you could get exactly the right exposure on a wall full of graffiti. That's not my idea of normal," Dennis concluded, a tinge of self-righteousness spiking his words.

"And you think that all my 'photographic abnormality' should end now, right?"

Warned by the hint of indignation in Kristin's voice, Dennis said soothingly, "Listen, Kris, you had your shot at it, at what you call 'serious' photography. Why would you want to keep banging your head against the wall? It doesn't appear that it's going to happen for you."

Kristin had an unearthly sense of feeling herself disappear. It was as if she'd known and shared herself with another person for a whole year and he had completely missed the most essential component of her being. She had fallen through the thin ice of their relationship.

"And what do you think *should* happen for me?" she asked, a tremor quirking her pulse.

After a pause for reflection, Dennis answered as soberly as the judge he intended to be one day. "I guess it's pretty obvious what I've been building up to with you. I mean, I've put in a major investment of time with you; it should be fairly clear that I'm looking at a long-range commitment. Provided, of course, that you're over your photography phase."

Kristin felt her stomach lurch. "My photography phase?" Her amazed disbelief was clear as she echoed Dennis's words.

"Come on, don't be offended. I know you take your work seriously, but so do I. These past few months haven't been a bed of roses for me either, you know. I mean, everyone down here at the firm knows we're dating. How do you think it looks for my girlfriend to be publicly panned like you were?"

Kristin dropped all pretense that she was working. "I don't know, Dennis, how *does* it look?" Her voice was cool and even.

"Pretty sorry, to be blunt about it. No one, but especially not an attorney, can afford to be associated with a loser." Hastily, he added, "I'm not saying that you're a loser, Kris, you know that. I'd never consider marrying a loser."

"Or someone with abnormal fixations on being a serious photographer. I guess I'm out on two counts then. Thanks for considering me. I think I'll withdraw my application. Good-bye, Dennis." With utmost delicacy, Kristin replaced the receiver. Mechanically, she went about finishing the charts while her mind reeled from the phone call.

This has definitely not been one of my better days, she thought with a numbed kind of detachment. The image of herself alone on a trail deep in the serene heart of a snowy forest appeared in her mind, a mental mirage of the oasis she yearned for now more than ever. The phone buzzed again. Kristin figured that it was Dennis calling back with a lawyerly explanation, an explanation that she no longer had any desire to hear.

Kristin opened Google and searched for the number of the Taos High Country Lodge. She hastily grabbed her own phone and was punching in the number listed for the lodge when she glanced up and found Mr. Pershing scrutinizing her, a severe look of disapproval creasing his pinched features. Kristin quickly hung up and Mr. Pershing strode into her cubicle.

"Kristin," he began in an acid tone, "if you would be so kind as to conduct your personal affairs on your own time and to confine your lunches to the allotted amount of time, I'm sure you'll get a lot more accomplished. Have you finished those charts yet?"

He moved to her monitor to ascertain for himself the answer to his question. Kristin fumbled to close the lodge's website. Instead, she accidentally closed her graphics program and the charts disappeared before she could save her work.

Kristin gasped, genuinely shocked that she'd inadvertently lost most of a day's work. More than anything else this latest symptom of the emotional turmoil she was undergoing alarmed her.

Her boss had noticed her error and was quick to berate her for it. "Why did you do that? Kristin, you need to get your head back in this game. You've had your opportunity for 'creative expression.'"

Another reference to her unsuccessful exhibit. How long would she have to put up with them?

Mr. Pershing continued in his tightly controlled, precise voice. "Productivity in this division has been way down for the past couple of months and a good bit of the reason for that has been your distraction."

"That is unfair," Kristin protested.

Mr. Pershing was stunned into silence for a moment; this was the first time Kristin had ever spoken back to him.

"The reason productivity is down is because we're short three artists. And the reason that it's not down even further than it is is because the other artists and I have been doing our work *and* the work of the three artists we're short."

"Is that so?" Mr. Pershing retorted peevishly.

Kristin knew that she had just destroyed any chance she might ever have for a raise, a promotion, or any kind of humane treatment as long as Pershing ruled Graphic Arts. He was a vindictive man who never forgot the slightest offense and she knew she had just offended him.

Kristin had watched the way he'd picked at anyone who affronted his thin-skinned sensibilities, hounding and overworking them until the hours from eight to five became unbearable. That was why the last three artists to leave had quit. It had been two months since Pershing had had a target for his nastiness. In a flash of insight, Kristin knew that if she stayed, she would become his next scapegoat. With equal clarity she tallied up the reasons she had for staying and came up with a balance of zero. Tracy was right; whether it was the ski-instructing job or something else, she needed to leave Albuquerque, to get away from all the reminders of her defeat, to recharge artistically, spiritually, and in every other way possible.

"I asked you a question, Jonsson," Mr. Pershing said threateningly. "You aren't answering it."

So it was "Jonsson" now. Kristin's suspicion was confirmed—she was already being marked as Pershing's next victim. Slowly, Kristin got to her feet and began pulling her prints off the cubicle wall. She stuffed them into the large tote she carried. They were followed by her personal art supplies, her coffee mug decorated with a ring of dancing bears, and a small African violet. Finally she turned to Pershing.

"I *am* answering your question, Mr. Pershing," Kristin said as she maneuvered around him with her large sack.

"What is the meaning of this?" he sputtered.

"Surely my actions are graphic enough for you," Kristin responded, somewhat pleased with her little pun and with the considerable style she'd just displayed in quitting.

Still, she thought as she stowed her tote bag alongside the rejected prints in the back of her car, *this has definitely* not *been one of my better days.*

Chapter 2

Kristin was amazed at how easy it had been to close down her life in Albuquerque. With just a few phone calls she'd located a friend to take over the lease on the house she rented. The friend had been delighted that most of the furnishings were to be left behind. All Kristin had packed, aside from the essentials, were her old hickory cross-country skis, an assortment of woolen clothing, and her photography equipment, which she'd stuffed in the bottom of a suitcase. She wasn't certain whether she'd ever want to see her Leica cameras and lenses again, much less use them. It was only her habit of optimism that made her bring them along.

The one item Kristin absolutely couldn't leave behind was Punkin', her golden retriever. The dog had earned her name because, as a pup, she'd been as round and orange as the Halloween favorite. Though she'd grown into a sturdy companion, always eager to accompany

Kristin on a mountain expedition or an in-city photo tour, Punkin' had retained both her jack-o'-lantern coloring and her playful puppy nature. She now sat quietly on the other side of the Volvo's front seat, watching the outskirts of Albuquerque slide past the window. They were on the road north, heading toward Taos to either start a new life or salvage an old one, Kristin hadn't made up her mind which.

"We're on the road again, Punkin' girl," Kristin said, ruffling the fur around the dog's shoulders. The retriever looked over her shoulder at her mistress. Her black lips were parted in the canine equivalent of a smile, almost as if Punkin' were remembering their last long trip together. That had been four years before, right after Kristin had been accepted into the University of New Mexico's graduate program in photography. She and Punkin' had driven down to New Mexico from Wisconsin. Kristin's mother had issued dire warnings when she'd made that move and she had echoed them the night before when Kristin called home with the news of her planned departure.

"What about that nice lawyer you've been seeing?" her mother had asked. "He's not going to wait around forever, you know, while you gallop all over the country trying to find yourself or whatever it is you're doing this time."

"I'm not asking him to wait," Kristin had explained patiently, not wanting to go into any further details on the subject. She'd long ago resigned herself to the fact that she was not the daughter her mother had hoped for, that she was not even one her mother could understand. To her mother it was incomprehensible that an unmarried woman would "throw away" a catch like an established attorney. And to do it the same day she quit a steady job, well, that was nothing short of lunacy. Kristin's real and sometimes urgent need to express herself dated back to when she was a little girl who'd tried to beautify her surroundings with crayon drawings on the wall and had always mystified Mrs. Jonsson and her gentle, silent husband.

"Kristin, you're twenty-seven years old," her mother reminded her, as if she might have lost count. "What about a home, a family, a husband?"

"Mom, I can't think about those things now. All I'm trying to do at the moment is maintain my mental health." Kristin attempted to lighten her half-serious answer with a laugh. But her mother was in no mood for levity.

"Why doesn't Julie ever have these mental-health problems?"

Kristin had stifled a groan of exasperation. Though she loved her older sister dearly, she was thoroughly weary of having Julie held up to her as a model of stability and success simply because she'd married a respectable businessman and proceeded to deliver three adorable grandchildren.

"I suppose you must have used up all your sanity genes on your first offspring," Kristin had quipped, "and just didn't have enough left over for me." Not surprisingly, her mother wasn't amused. Kristin had ended the conversation by saying that she would call or text when she was settled.

Kristin's attention was recaptured by her immediate surroundings as she cut through the high mesa land outside of Santa Fe. She felt she could breathe again as the cluster of the city gave way to juniper-dotted hills that seemed to roll for a hundred miles in either direction until they lapped onto the base of one of the cobalt-blue mountain ranges ringing the area.

A surge of an emotion that, for Kristin, came close to a genuinely religious feeling shot through her as she was enraptured by the way the morning light lent the hills a mauve radiance. It was the quality of the light, its luminescent clarity, that had initially caused Kristin to fall in love with New Mexico. She was cheered by the emotion. *Tracy was right,* she thought to herself with a deep satisfaction, *I did need to get away from all the reminders that were closing in on me.*

In Santa Fe, Kristin wove her way around the tangle of winding streets that twisted through the four-hundred-year-old capital. For a few moments, she was tempted to stop and make a quick perusal of a couple of the galleries that typically featured photography. But she was anxious to be on her way, an anxiousness that had started with her one phone conversation with Grayson Lowrey. She had called the owner of the High Country Lodge as soon as she'd arrived home after quitting her job.

His voice had been deep and gravelly, and she'd pictured Mr. Grayson Lowrey as some gruff, woodsy character in a plaid flannel shirt and bushy brows beetling over his eyes—a Paul Bunyan of the Sangre de Cristos. He'd informed her, after a bare minimum of pleasantries, that, yes, they did have an instructor position open, adding, "But, you can hardly expect me to hire you over the phone."

Kristin had replied that, of course, she had expected nothing of the kind and that she'd be only too happy to drive up to High Country for an interview.

"Better make it before noon," Lowrey had growled. "After that you're not liable to catch me here, and I insist on personally interviewing every applicant."

Kristin agreed, but she had already made up her mind that she intended to have more than an interview.

Her old tan Volvo slowed down as they hit the steady rise that would eventually take them nine thousand feet up into the Sangre de Cristo Mountains. Even this early in the season their peaks were crowned in white. At the sight of the rugged mountains that, four centuries earlier, had marked the northernmost limits of the Spanish conquistadores' dominion, something stirred within Kristin that had lain dormant over the long summer. It was the special affinity she had with nature, particularly a snow-capped nature. That love was her legacy from her father and had been nurtured in her childhood growing up in Wisconsin, where, at least for her, camping and other outdoor activities hadn't drawn to a close at the end of an all-too-brief summer.

Kristin thought of the countless times in the middle of a frozen Wisconsin winter when she'd backpacked into a deserted camping area for an overnight trip with her father and, more often than not, a troop of Boy Scouts. Reflecting on it now, she realized that her love of the snowy wilderness probably was born out of a deep need to make some kind of contact with her kind yet distant and undemonstrative father. Their outings had been the only time that they had shared.

Kristin shook her head philosophically. So Julie had been the daughter her mother had always wanted and she, Kristin, had attempted to be the son her father never had. In a way it was sad, but Kristin chose not to mourn for the love her father had withheld. Instead she felt a strong gratitude for what he had been able to give her.

"We're good scouts, aren't we, Punkin'?" she said, reaching out to pat the patient, furry head beside her. The dog looked at her, dropped her lower jaw, and panted heartily to acknowledge that she enjoyed being included in Kristin's reveries.

"And we're going to prove it to this Mr. Grayson Lowrey, this Paul Bunyan of the Sangre de Cristos." Kristin had fully made up her mind: She wanted that job. More than that, she needed it. Needed to the depths of her soul the solace and the beauty of the mountains that the job could offer.

A feed store, the Kit Carson Drive-In, and the Sun God motel welcomed Kristin to Taos. With the realization of exactly how much the High Country position meant to her, Kristin reappraised her outfit—a pair of old jeans, somewhat worn at the knees, and a wine-colored sweater—and found it lacking. She pulled off the road into a gas station, where the teenaged attendant insisted on pumping her gas for her while she went around to the back of the car and dug through her suitcase in search of a more impressive interview ensemble.

The best she could come up with was a slightly nicer pair of jeans and the black cashmere sweater her mother had sent for her last birthday. Kristin ducked into the restroom to change and examined herself in the scarred mirror. Not bad, she decided, but since this was an interview for a position where she would be meeting and working with lodge guests, she still needed a bit more polish. For this she pulled out her meager stock of cosmetics.

She outlined her gray-flecked green eyes in sable brown and darkened her long, cinnamon-colored lashes.

A few strokes of blusher and a swipe of lip gloss completed her makeup routine. Then she unbraided the thick rope of flame-colored hair trailing down her back. It crackled as she ran a brush briskly through it. Freed from its customary braid, Kristin's mane bounced and gleamed, framing her face with waves and copper highlights. Just to give herself a shred more confidence, she spritzed her neck and wrists with her favorite perfume, a light, spicy concoction.

"Well, that's the best I can do under the circumstances," she said to her own reflection, hoping that her best would prove to be good enough for the gravel-voiced Mr. Grayson Lowrey.

As she walked back out to the car, the adolescent attendant caught sight of Kristin and his hand froze on the gas pump.

"Hey," Kristin called out, laughing, "watch out."

The teenager snapped out of his momentary trance and looked down to where she was pointing. Gas had overflowed Kristin's tank and was running down the side of her car.

"Oh, jeez," he stammered, clicking the pump off and whipping out the dirty rag in his back pocket to wipe up the overflow. Kristin pulled a paper towel from the dispenser above the gas pump and helped him mop up.

"Wow, thanks," he gulped as she helped him clean

off the side of the Volvo. "You don't have to pay for the spilled gas or nothin'."

Kristin smiled at his largesse.

"I mean, I'll pay for it. Or no one has to pay for it. Forget it," he stammered, beginning to flush a sweaty red under Kristin's gaze. "It's on the house."

"Say," Kristin asked, hoping to divert the teenager from his own embarrassment, "could you tell me how to find the High Country Lodge?"

"Sure. You bet," came the eager response, followed by a set of directions. "You going to stay up there?"

Kristin nodded, not wanting to go into a lengthy explanation of her mission.

"People tell me it's great. They come back every year. I know a fellow who used to work up there; says the head guy, Lowrey, really knows how to run a first-class operation."

"That's good to know," Kristin said sincerely, handing the boy a few bills to pay for the gas both in and around her tank.

The route to High Country Lodge took Kristin and Punkin' past wide-open pastures that were lightly frosted with the remnants of an early snow. Black-and-white magpies swooped over the fields where cattle and, in one instance, shaggy buffalo grazed oblivious to the pestering birds. Like silent giants, the Sangre de Cristos closed in around the Volvo, and before Kristin was even aware of it, she was in the mountains.

She was alerted to the fact that she'd arrived when she spotted her first grove of aspens. Kristin considered the lovely trees to be a kind of mountain sentry guarding the high slopes. They always gave an impression of vigilance with their ruler-straight trunks and leaves that quaked with even the slightest breeze. She pulled off into a roadside campground with a stream coursing through it and let Punkin' out for a romp.

The tangerine-toned dog galloped off after a Steller's jay that had dive-bombed her as soon as she poked her head out. She splashed happily through the stream, delirious to be in an environment she loved as much as Kristin did. Fifteen minutes later, Kristin spread Punkin's special blanket over her half of the front seat and called to the dog. Punkin' came immediately, stopped at Kristin's feet, and looked up at her mistress with a thoroughly confused expression. Usually when she was let out of the car in the mountains, it meant that she and Kristin were going on a long hike and she could look forward to a day, or even a couple of days, of outdoor frolicking.

"Come on," Kristin said, chuckling at the expression on the bewildered retriever's face, "into the car. You'll get more than enough of these mountains before the winter's over."

High Country Lodge was larger than Kristin had

expected. It looked like an Alpine chalet with its steeply pitched roof, window boxes of hearty geraniums, and carved wooden shutters. It was two stories high and Kristin noticed solar collectors attached to an inconspicuous part of the roof. *At least this Grayson Lowrey's heart is in the right place*, Kristin thought, approving of the lodge owner's interest in alternative energy. After settling Punkin' down for a short nap on her blanket, Kristin tromped over the patches of snow up the front walk to the open door.

Inside, the lodge was permeated with the wonderful scent from countless fires of tangy piñon wood that had been built in the large fireplace dominating the main room. Kristin had a fleeting vision of herself, weary from a day of skiing, sitting around a roaring fire, enjoying the convivial company of a few lodge guests. The walls were paneled in varnished pine, and thick scatter rugs were strewn over a tiled floor. Built-in benches encircled the brick fireplace. A high, vaulted ceiling arced overhead.

But what struck Kristin most strongly was the noise. Sounds of hammering, sawing, and vacuuming greeted her as she entered the lodge's main room. A stocky middle-aged woman carrying a pail of soapy water and a scrub brush bustled past.

"Excuse me," Kristin called after her.

The woman, her hair hidden beneath a bandanna, halted and turned back around. "I'm sorry," she apologized, a twangy accent betraying her country origins. "We're all so absorbed in getting ready to open up that I didn't notice you. What can I do for you?" A smile lightened her broad face.

"I'm looking for Mr. Grayson Lowrey."

"Oh, you mean Gray. He should be in his office. Just take those stairs off to the right and you'll find the boss behind the first door you come to."

"Thanks," Kristin said, instinctively liking the woman and encouraged by the fact that High Country's owner was just "Gray" to her.

At the top of the stairs, Kristin paused, ran a slightly trembling hand over her hair, and knocked.

"It's open." The voice was just as gruff as it had been over the phone.

Kristin pushed open the door and found herself face-to-face with Grayson Lowrey. He appeared to be both what she had expected and the farthest thing from her preconceptions. He certainly was a woodsy type, right down to the plaid flannel shirt she'd anticipated. But he was considerably younger than the old codger she'd imagined. Midthirties was Kristin's instantaneous calculation. And there were certainly no beetling brows.

Before Kristin could even pluck one feature out from another, everything, the color of his eyes, the angle of his nose, the sweep of his brow, all blended together into one highly unsettling presence. It was a presence that was overwhelmingly masculine—from the pair of broad shoulders that loomed above the desk he sat behind to the neatly trimmed beard sprinkled with gray curling above an improbably expansive chest. Kristin attempted to rein in her turmoiled reaction by reminding herself that she had *never* been attracted to the brawny type. Lean, sensitive artists and cerebral lawyers had always been more to her taste.

"Yes?" He glanced up, the fountain pen in his hand poised above the documents scattered across the top of his oversized antique desk. On the walls were several Two Gray Hills Indian rugs done in traditional geometric patterns of gray and red. Some recessed niches held the distinctive black pottery of the San Ildefonso pueblo. The pen was slowly lowered as Grayson Lowrey made a more complete appraisal of his visitor. His coffee-brown eyes warmed in a way that disconcerted Kristin even further.

"Yes, hello." She held out her hand, then retracted it jerkily. The poise she had been so carefully mustering only a moment before was now scattered to the wind. "I'm Kristin Jonsson." Her announcement was received with a blank stare. Nerves goaded Kristin into babbling on foolishly. "That's with two *s*'s and no *h*." The full mouth above the gray-dappled brown beard curved with barely suppressed amusement. "I spoke to you about interviewing for the instructor/guide position."

The slow-blooming smile abruptly disappeared.

"'Instructor/guide'?" He echoed her words questioningly, as if he hadn't fully understood them.

Kristin's heart sank. "You haven't already found someone, have you?"

"No, the job's still open."

The low-pitched timbre of his bass voice rumbled through Kristin. She couldn't help noticing that his initial glimmer of friendliness had vanished the moment she'd expressed her interest in working for him as an instructor. He looked away from her and studied the finely wrought gold pen that he now held between two large hands as intently as he had been studying her a moment before. She watched in silence as he twirled the pen. The rough masculinity of his work-hardened hands was emphasized by an exquisitely crafted silver bracelet set with three nuggets of pale-green turquoise webbed in a dark charcoal. Kristin noted the superb taste he displayed in his office furnishings and jewelry. That and his manner of polished control were both at odds with the Paul Bunyan bumpkin persona she'd preconceived.

"Is there any problem then with my applying for the vacancy?" she asked, breaking a silence that had grown uncomfortably long.

After another lengthy pause, Grayson Lowrey finally looked up and spoke. "To be quite frank with you, I'd expected someone a bit different. I thought you were here to ask about hostess or cocktail waitress jobs at Powderhorn."

"'Cocktail waitress'?" It was Kristin's turn now to echo his words in disbelief. "At a downhill ski resort?" She found both categories unthinkable. "No, I'd like to work here, at High Country." She corrected him as calmly as she possibly could.

"I see," he said, letting the pen drop. "Have a seat and tell me about yourself. Have you ever taught cross-country skiing before?"

Kristin settled into a comfortable leather armchair opposite the desk. At least she was ready for his first question and told him about her countless expeditions with her father and his Boy Scout troops, emphasizing that, typically, out of a dozen scouts, perhaps one or two would have ever been on touring skis before. "By the end of the day, though, we had every one of those boys skiing as easily as he walked," she recalled, proud of the new dimension she'd been able to add to young lives.

Grayson Lowrey merely nodded noncommittally and made a note on the pad in front of him. Kristin felt as if his attention were a thousand miles away. She struggled to reclaim it.

"I mean," she dove in, "cross-country *is* as natural as walking, isn't it? The basis of the ski motion is just an extended stride with more pronounced arm movements."

He nodded again in silent agreement with her analysis, yet Kristin could feel him, for some reason she couldn't fathom, mentally slipping away. She feared that he had already eliminated her as a serious candidate.

Fired with the determination not to endure yet another psychic defeat, Kristin began chronicling all her wilderness experience. Starting with her childhood in Wisconsin, she moved on to her more recent adventures skiing in the Sandia Mountains outside of Albuquerque. "Then, just last Christmas," she continued breathlessly, "I took off with the Sierra Club for some backcountry ski mountaineering in Utah. And that Thanksgiving a friend and I . . ."

"Whoa," the man behind the desk called out, holding up his hand, the hint of a smile flirting at the corners of his mouth. "You sound like you've been filling in for Smokey the Bear."

Nervousness and relief peppered Kristin's laugh. "I just want you to know that I'm qualified."

"That's a difficult thing to ascertain with a job like this. High Country instructors do more than just teach students how to make their skis slide forward and take guests to scenic spots. They're responsible for lives." Lowrey stretched a long arm behind him in the direction of a window that faced onto a forbiddingly steep summit. "Those mountains are beautiful in a way that I can't even begin to describe, but they can kill the unwary. They can bury a person with a ton of snow, freeze him to death, or crack away at the wrong moment and send him tumbling to his death."

"Mr. Lowrey"—Kristin felt compelled to speak, to puncture a hole in the airtight case he seemed to be building against her—"we have avalanches, subzero weather, and rockslides in Wisconsin. I've also dealt with all three in the mountains around Albuquerque. What sort of proof of competency do you generally require from your applicants?"

"Most I know personally or are recommended to me. But usually I rely heavily on my own perceptions about a person."

"And you perceived me to be a cocktail waitress, right?" Kristin asked dispiritedly.

"Look, it's not that I don't think women can make fine instructors. Some of the best I've had have been female. But they have to be a special kind of woman. Not the kind who'll be afraid to help a beginner with his binding for fear of mussing up her manicure. Not the kind who'll expect some hero to come along and bail her out of a crisis. I can't have that, not when lives depend on the people I hire."

Kristin was startled by the vehemence with which Lowrey expressed his opinions. She also began to suspect what had triggered them. "Mr. Lowrey, I think you might have gotten a mistaken impression of me. I'm not someone who worries overly much about her manicure. I don't even usually wear makeup, and my characteristic hairdo is a braid down the back."

As he held his silence, Kristin studied his features beneath the unruly shock of sun-streaked brown hair that topped them. It appeared that his sturdy, slightly crooked nose had been broken at some time in what was obviously a vigorously athletic past. Even beneath the beard, his facial bones made themselves felt with a hard, angular authority. The unrelieved ruggedness of his face, however, seemed almost at odds with the warmth of his brown eyes. They were misplaced above the jutting thrust of his cheekbones. For a brief moment, Kristin saw the flicker of an immense vulnerability in their mahogany depths, but she quickly corrected that notion as the twin orbs visibly froze against her.

"I'm sorry, Miss Jonsson," he said, a chilly brusqueness creeping into his tone, "but I really don't think it would work out. If you'd like to apply for something at Powderhorn, I'll give you the name of my personnel director there and will phone in a strong recommendation on your behalf." It was obvious that Lowrey considered the interview concluded as he bent over his paperwork.

Kristin bit down on the inside of her lip to stanch the flow of tears she felt surging to her eyes. "I really want that job." Her voice was tight and low as she fought to keep even the slightest hint of a quiver out of it. "I don't think you should eliminate me without a fair trial." With the thought *What have I got to lose?* exploding in the back of her mind, she blurted out, "I challenge you to a night on that mountain."

"You what?"

Kristin had succeeded at last in claiming his full and undivided attention.

With somewhat less bravado, she indicated the peak visible from the window behind Lowrey and reissued her dare. "I challenge you to a night on that mountain."

"A night? On Diablo Peak?" he quizzed. "Do you have any idea of how rough it is up there? It's over twelve thousand feet at the summit and snow-packed year-round. I would never think of taking guests up there overnight." He stopped for a moment, teetering on the verge of dismissing both Kristin and her challenge. Then an indefinable gleam animated his countenance. It contained a spark of something that Kristin couldn't analyze, but it left her feeling both newly hopeful and a little afraid. "But if you can make it anywhere close to the top of Diablo on skis," Lowrey concluded, "you've got a job."

A rush of exuberance flooded through Kristin. In the next instant, it was soured by a trickle of doubt. Could she do it? Was she in good enough physical condition? She quickly dammed up any flow of doubt, though, when she saw the smug expression on Grayson Lowrey's face, an expression that told her how supremely confident he was that she would fail. Kristin decided that wiping the arrogant assurance off his face would be as much a reward as securing the job. In the meantime, she had quite a lot of preparing to do.

"For the purposes of this"—Lowrey paused, arching his eyebrow—"'tryout,' I'll pretend to be precisely what your typical client would be, a helpless novice."

"I was going to suggest that very arrangement," Kristin concurred, her irritation showing as the gray flecks in her green eyes turned to chips of granite. "I'll handle all the preparation, including mapping the route we will follow."

"Excellent. Then shall we meet back here, ready to go at . . ." He stopped and deferred to Kristin, allowing her to set their departure time.

"Seven too early for you?"

"Not in the least. I'd suggest, though, that you stay here at the lodge tonight."

"That won't be necessary," Kristin replied stiffly, remembering the little aspen-enclosed campground where Punkin' had romped on the way up. She much preferred a night in her trusty pup tent to accepting Grayson Lowrey's hospitality.

"Suit yourself," Lowrey conceded.

"I intend to," Kristin said, marshaling every shred of dignity she could and rising regally to her feet. In that instant, while she loomed above Grayson Lowrey, she was thankful for every centimeter of her height, for every inch from which it allowed her to look down on him.

Then Lowrey too rose to his feet, and Kristin's momentary advantage was lost. *My God*, she thought, experiencing the rare sensation of being towered over by a man by a good half a foot, *he* is *the Paul Bunyan of the Sangre de Cristos.* She supposed she should have guessed it from the size of his shoulders, but it would have been hard to imagine a body so massively in proportion. She refused to allow her surprise to communicate itself and concluded their first meeting with a cool, "Until tomorrow."

"I'll be looking forward to it, Miss Jonsson."

His lightly mocking tone was not lost on her. As she shut the office door behind her, Kristin swore to herself that, even if she had to drag herself up the side of that mountain by sheer willpower alone, by the end of the following day *she* would be the one with a smirk on her face.

Chapter 3

***H**ow'd it go?"*

Kristin was so lost in her plans for the next day's expedition that the cheery woman to whom she had spoken on her way upstairs had to ask twice before she could penetrate the wall of Kristin's absorption.

"The interview," the woman clarified. "I reckoned that you were talking to Gray about a job." She paused and clucked her tongue as if scolding herself for her boldness. "But you're probably not inclined to go around handing out the details of your life to every stranger who asks; I know I'm not." The ruddy-faced woman held out a hand, still slightly moist from wash water. "I'm Addie Watkins, chief cook and canteen washer during the off-season. When things start swinging, I'm supposed to be in charge, managing them for Gray."

Kristin returned the introduction. Then, unable to

resist the woman's merry affability, she added, "To be honest, the interview didn't go all that well."

Addie bunched her eyebrows together as if she were puzzling over a mystery she couldn't quite solve. "Funny, I could almost have predicted that."

"Why?" Kristin asked, feeling as though she were the object of some elaborate inside joke. "Is everyone around here judged on external appearance?"

"It would seem, at least as far as Gray and good-looking female instructors go, that's the case. So you didn't get the job?"

"He hasn't decided yet," Kristin confided. "We're going to ski Diablo tomorrow."

"Diablo, eh," the woman said, clearly impressed by Kristin's pluck. "Sort of an audition?"

Kristin nodded, her fears of proving inadequate surfacing in a sudden glumness.

Addie noticed Kristin's insecurity and tried to bolster her confidence by offering to pack her a lunch for the trail. Kristin readily agreed, pleased to have at least one detail taken care of. "I'll leave out some of my home-baked streusel to get you going in the morning." Even better than the two meals, though, Addie said she'd be "tickled" to look after Punkin' for the day.

"No trouble at all," Addie insisted. "Good luck," she called after Kristin as her long strides carried her out to the Volvo. She had a lot to accomplish and not much time in which to get it all done. In Taos, she found a wilderness-supply store that sold topographical maps, and she purchased one that detailed the contours of Diablo Peak. She studied it avidly. Her father had taught her how to translate the swirling lines into the hills and valleys they represented. She planned to chart a route with which Grayson Lowrey would be unable to find any fault. After purchasing the few items of gear she hadn't brought with her from Albuquerque, Kristin headed back up to the campground.

Between preparing a one-pot dinner over a butane cooking stove and tossing a stick untold times for the indefatigable Punkin' to retrieve, Kristin managed to get ready for the next day's ordeal. She located and packed all of what her father always called contingency gear. "You might not need all this folderol on your ordinary tramp through the wilds," she could remember her father warning in his characteristically terse way as he dipped matches in paraffin to waterproof them and made sure that the antivenin serum in his snakebite kit was still fresh, "but on your out-of-the-ordinary trip, the one you've always got to be ready for, it'll save your life." Although the temperature dipped into the high teens during the night, Kristin stayed snug and cozy in her goosedown-filled bag, its warmth augmented by Punkin's abundant natural supply.

The first streaks of crimson were cracking a

night-dark sky when Kristin headed up to the High Country Lodge. The sight of the lodge unloosed the butterflies in her stomach that Kristin had been struggling to keep grounded. But her nervousness didn't center entirely around the day's trek; the fluttering seemed to worsen as she remembered the sensation of Grayson Lowrey towering above her.

Kristin sternly reminded herself once again that such specimens of overgrown muscularity had never appealed to her. He was probably one of those lunks, she decided curtly, who'd had all the sensitivity battered out of him on a football field. She refused to listen to the small contradictory voice that attempted to remind her that an insensitive lunk wouldn't have chosen the rugs, pottery, and jewelry she'd seen in Grayson Lowrey's office. Nor would he have manifested even the fleeting glimpse of vulnerability Kristin had seen in his eyes. Or thought that she'd seen.

Punkin' bounded from the car when Kristin got out to unlatch the rack on the roof that held her skis. She herded the dog inside the lodge, found a thick rug, and put Punkin' and her favorite tattered old blanket down on it. Kristin was pleased to find that no one else was up. It boosted her confidence to think that she'd managed to be there and ready before the Paul Bunyan of the Sangre de Cristos. Out in the kitchen she spotted the lunch and breakfast Addie had promised, and she stowed the lunch bag in her backpack. Though she didn't feel like eating anything, she knew she would need the energy before long and cut herself a slice of Addie's yeasty streusel.

"How about a cup of coffee to go with that?" Lowrey's voice seemed to have been switched on in the kitchen like the low-throated hum of a generator.

"That would be nice," Kristin answered, her edge of confidence shattering at the sight of Lowrey nearly filling the doorframe with a pair of powerful shoulders that stretched the cream-colored fisherman's knit sweater he wore. His slender hips were clad in jeans that swelled with the bulk of a skier's well-developed thighs. Somehow Lowrey seemed much more approachable this morning, almost as if Kristin had caught him in a state of sleepy innocence before he'd fully awakened and been rudely abraded by all the day's problems. As he moved to the sink to attend to the domestic chore, carefully filling a blue-speckled enameled pot with water and placing it delicately on one of the eight burners on the restaurant-sized stove, Kristin was inexplicably touched by his cautious grace. He seemed aware of his size and power and of his constant responsibility to keep both in check.

"Hope you don't mind cowboy coffee," he said, throwing a handful of grounds into the water.

Kristin laughed; she hadn't heard that expression in years. "I had ample opportunity to acquire a taste for that particular brew," she confessed. "That was the only way my father knew how to make coffee over a campfire. Consequently, that was how I first learned to drink it, years before my mother would allow me to touch the stuff at home."

Lowrey chuckled companionably, and Kristin's apprehensions about the day began to dissolve. As they took their streusel and coffee to the dining room and sat at one of the five long tables hewn from polished cedar, it seemed to her that he almost was looking forward to the outing.

"You look a lot more like a mountain person today," Lowrey observed, eyeing her outfit a bit more closely than Kristin thought absolutely necessary to determine its mountain-worthiness. She was wearing a snug-fitting powder-blue turtleneck tucked into the waistband of tweed knickers. A pair of knee socks with a snowflake design woven into their sides closed the gap between her knickers and low-topped ski boots. Lowrey's gaze made her acutely aware that the wide suspenders she was wearing pressed against the generous mounds of her breasts.

"Were you expecting me to show up in spike heels and gold lamé?" Kristin teased.

"I was a bit brusque yesterday," Lowrey admitted, stirring a rich trickle of cream into his coffee. "I'm sorry." Again that flash of infinite vulnerability flooded his eyes. Those eyes communicated so much more than his words that Kristin found it difficult to follow the surface conversation; she was trying so hard to fathom what was behind them. Much as it galled her, she could not deny that she was drawn to this man. Given his compellingly masculine presence and his ownership of several ski resorts, Kristin had no doubt that her attraction was not a unique phenomenon. How many other women, she wondered, had tried to decipher the cryptic message encoded in Grayson Lowrey's eyes?

"No, I can understand your concern," she said, once she'd reined in her stampeding speculations. Unable to either understand or sustain the moment they seemed to be sharing, Kristin broke it. "Guess we'd better head for the hills," she suggested lamely. She instantly regretted her glibness, for it destroyed Lowrey's mood of easy companionability and reawakened the crusty outdoors entrepreneur she'd encountered the day before.

"Let's go then," he growled.

Outside, Lowrey sauntered away from the lodge with an athletic grace. Shafts of morning light silhouetted him against the dawn-purpled mountains. The artist in Kristin thrilled to the sight of a man of Lowrey's heroic proportions cast against such a fittingly majestic backdrop. She immediately squelched that response and focused on the task at hand, knowing that their journey had begun. From now on her every movement would be scrutinized and judged.

True to his word, Lowrey hung back, offering no assistance as he played the role of complete novice and waited for Kristin to do everything for both of them. Without a word she entered into the charade, checking his skis and helping him shoulder his backpack. Then she unfolded her topo map and went over the route she'd mapped out, just as she had always done with the scouts so that they would become more involved, more a part of the adventure.

Feeling like an actress and hoping that she was reading the correct lines, Kristin said, "We'll hike in to where the real snow is, then wax when we know what the conditions are."

She took Lowrey's nod to mean that he approved, that she had performed adequately on the preliminaries. With that they set off. The trail rose steeply, quickly enfolding them in a cool, evergreen world. The kind of profound solitude that can only be experienced in a forest in winter claimed Kristin's soul and she gave it up gladly. As much as she delighted in backpacking during the warm summer months, winter outings—when the trails were deserted by the noisy hordes and a mantle of snow muffled all sounds except the melancholy tune played by the wind as it teased the treetops—were her true love. As they ascended, the sporadic patches of snow gave way to a dense cover.

When they reached a level clearing, Kristin bent over and balled up a handful of the frosty stuff in her glove.

The way it clumped together, or failed to, would tell her what kind of wax they needed to rub into the bottoms of their skis. The snow was old but still fairly dry and powdery, thanks to the low temperatures at that altitude. She considered her choice of wax far longer than she normally would have, knowing that Lowrey was waiting to pass judgment on the selection she made.

"Normally," she said, trying to sound assured and confident, "I would recommend blue wax with a purple kicker, but since the trail is so steep, we'll go with a softer wax to give us more traction uphill and to slow us down on the descents."

Like the beginner he was pretending to be, Lowrey made no comment; he merely accepted the decision the way a trusting novice would have. Always before, Kristin had had the benefit of her father's counsel, either approving or vetoing her decisions. Lowrey's unquestioning compliance brought home his point about the burden of responsibility an instructor bore with far more impact than any lecture ever could have. As Kristin dug into her pack for the right wax, she wondered what the consequences would be if she had made the wrong choice. She found the chocolate-colored stick of wax about the size and shape of a tube of blusher, peeled back its thin tin shell, and crayoned two streaks down the bottoms of her skis. Next she smoothed the wax down with a piece of cork that fit in the palm of her hand.

"Waxing," Kristin explained, "allows the skis to grip the snow crystals when we're going uphill and to glide over them when we're going down."

Lowrey, still playing the ignorant novice, piped up in a comically shrill voice. "And how is it possible for the wax to do both, Madam Instructress?"

Kristin could not resist a smile as she played along. "That's a very good question, Mr. Lowrey. It's a matter of simple physics. Fresh snowflakes are spiked, like the crystals you see on your window on winter mornings. These spikes are anchors when you put your weight on your skis. That's where the wax comes in. It's full of tiny holes the spikes stick to. Once you've pushed off, you're not actually skiing on the snow. With momentum, you're skimming along on a layer of water created by friction between ski and snow."

Although Lowrey nodded with a mock sageness, Kristin hoped that he approved of the explanation she would have given to a beginning skier.

She passed the wax and cork to Lowrey, who, momentarily, dropped the pretense of ignorance. His back to Kristin, he stretched one extravagantly long arm up to support the tip of his ski while he smeared on the wax. The muscles of his shoulders and lower torso came to life, rippling beneath the sweater as he labored over the ski, rubbing the wax in with a few deft strokes of the cork. Kristin was surprised by the fluid, almost balletic grace with which he moved. It was completely unexpected in someone she'd dismissed as a muscle-bound lunk.

"How's it look, Teach?" Lowrey joked, holding up his perfectly waxed ski bottom for her inspection.

"It'll do, son," she joked back, happy that a lighter mood had been recaptured.

It was clear that Lowrey was too eager to attack the trail to keep up his role as Kristin's student. He clamped his skis onto his boots and pushed off with one mighty thrust from his poles. Just as he had looked so right silhouetted against a mountain backdrop, he seemed completely in his element in motion on skis. Watching him, Kristin thought of a snow leopard moving effortlessly across a whitened landscape. Coils of muscle bunched at the backs of his thighs and shoulders, then exploded into motion, propelling him in smooth bursts across the snow. He skied like a champion, leaning forward and vigorously stabbing the snow base ahead, digging his pole in, kicking off with the ski on the opposite side, and gliding forward. *Stab, kick, glide.* The mesmerizing rhythm quickly took Lowrey out of view, and Kristin had to scramble to catch up.

The edge of the flat clearing was clotted with bushy pines, funneling the skiers back onto the steep trail. As she began the uphill climb, Kristin was gratified to discover that her skis held; they didn't let her slip back downhill. Her choice of wax had been correct. That was the last pleasant thought she had time to enjoy, however, for the incline rapidly took its toll. After a few minutes her lungs began to burn and breathing became labored.

The first mile is the toughest, she told herself, repeating the axiom that kept runners and cross-country skiers alike going while their bodies adjusted, or attempted to adjust, to the inordinate demands both sports made upon them. The muscles at the backs of her legs were the first to call attention to themselves, a call that Kristin was determined to ignore. Her exhalations trailed behind her in frosty white plumes like the steam from a locomotive. Still she pushed on, goaded forward by a glimpse of Lowrey's electric-blue backpack disappearing around the corner of one of the switchbacks that zigzagged up the mountain.

Kristin blotted out all thoughts except keeping up, not allowing that backpack to escape any farther. She forgot everything else—the forest around her, the snow yielding beneath her skis, her overtaxed lungs, her complaining legs, her aching shoulders—and plunged forward, deeper and higher, into the shadowy fastness of Diablo Peak.

So intense was her concentration that Kristin almost ran over Lowrey before she became aware of him, poised at the edge of a clearing, studying her progress.

"Kristin Jonsson, with two *s*'s," he proclaimed as she neared him, "you surprise me. There aren't many who could have kept up with the pace I set. Excuse me, this is really my first all-out trip of the season and I let my exuberance get the better of me."

Kristin was too winded to speak for the moment, so she merely held up a hand to indicate her forgiveness. Lowrey's words of praise, however, acted on her like an oxygen mask, suffusing her with a renewed source of energy.

"Come on over this way," he said, striking off from the trail. "I think you might like this view."

"Like" proved to be a vast understatement. The sunny clearing opened onto a view of the valley with High Country Lodge at its base far below. Kristin was astounded at the altitude they'd gained in such a short time. They were high enough that the vista unfolding below them was a dramatic panorama. Rusty sunlight froze the Taos valley in gilded amber. A rich blue haze of piñon and cedar smoke hung over the awakening village. To the east, the black slash of the Rio Grande gorge snaked its way across the expanse of the sagebrush mesa. Kristin and Grayson Lowrey stood, side by side, transfixed by the sheer power and sweep of the snow gullied country at their feet.

As she had earlier that morning, Kristin again experienced a profound sense of kinship with Lowrey. Without turning her head, she glanced sideways at him and had the startling sensation of feeling time slip away from her.

The profile she glimpsed could have come straight out of a history book about the mountain men who, a century and a half ago, had roamed these high wildernesses, hunting and trapping. Lowrey had that same untamable quality about him, that same vastness of spirit that would never feel entirely at home any place where an infinity of rugged terrain didn't stretch out around him for miles in every direction. In silent communion, they shared the intense feelings they both had for the land.

They were so quiet and still that a snowshoe rabbit, only halfway done with his annual metamorphosis from his camouflaging summer brown to winter white, hopped nonchalantly past them, so close that they could see the twitching of his whiskers. Lowrey smiled at the small animal like a benevolent god pleased with his tiny creation.

As he turned to Kristin, his bemusement-gentled features came into a crisper focus and he asked, "Do you want to lead off?"

Kristin poled slowly away from the sunny clearing in answer to his question.

"May I make one suggestion?" he asked, following her. "Relax. Your form is impeccable, but you could double your endurance if you were less tense and let yourself flow with the motion of the skis."

Kristin knew that the suggestion was a valid one. In the next few minutes, she regained her affinity with nature and skiing was once again the fluid joy it had always been. Gliding over the snow, in tune now with both her skis and her surroundings, she became aware of the gurgling of a nearby brook and the way the bristlecone pines seemed to be curtsying as they sloughed off the overloaded shawls of white snow wrapped about their branches. A hoarse, raucous cry caught her attention. Overhead, a pair of ravens wheeled through the sapphire-blue sky, their black plumage glistening with purple highlights in the sun's rays. She breathed in, filling her lungs with the kind of air she had longed for during those stuffy months when she was cooped up in the airless office she had left in Albuquerque.

That memory, the thought of going back to a place like the Graphic Arts Division, spurred Kristin on. She recognized that, eventually, she would have to return to a commercial art job. *But not now*, she pleaded silently. *Not until I've healed.* Stopping only occasionally to check her map and to down a swallow of water from the canteen at her hip, she moved steadily upward, sliding noiselessly through the shadowy forest. Bit by bit the dense growth of spruce and fir trees gave way to occasional sunlit patches. The conifers continued to thin out until a nearly unobstructed view of the summit was visible. Diablo Peak thrust into the sky with a craggy defiance.

At last, they broke through; they were above timberline. The unshaded sun beat down on Kristin with a welcome warmth. She stripped off her parka and stuffed it into her pack.

"Feels good, doesn't it?" Lowrey asked, following Kristin's lead and removing his nubby sweater.

"Yes, it's exquisite," she agreed as his head disappeared inside the bulky sweater and his chest came into view. He was wearing thermal underwear that hugged the mounded contours of his body. Kristin was surprised by how lean he actually was beneath the thick sweater. The breadth of his shoulders had made him appear heavier than he was. Under the twin swells of his shoulders and chest his stomach appeared as hard and flat as a manhole cover. She had the same reaction to his superbly conditioned torso that she had to an exceptionally well-executed piece of sculpture: She wanted very badly to touch it. Stifling the unthinkable urge, Kristin looked away quickly as he finished tugging the sweater over his head.

"Not too much farther to go," she said, pretending to have been studying the peak ahead.

"We've made remarkable time," Lowrey commented. "How about lunch? I know the perfect spot."

At the mention of the word, Kristin became aware of just how hungry she was. Addie's breakfast streusel had been spent in energy output long ago. They both removed their skis and attached them to their packs, because there was little snow on the sunny meadow and they could hike the remaining distance. Lowrey led them to a south-facing culvert that was protected from the ceaseless winds that raked the mountain above timberline. At first Kristin thought she was hallucinating; the spot was alive with wildflowers.

"My God," she gasped, collapsing onto the flowered earth, "you've discovered Shangri-la."

"Not quite," Lowrey demurred as he joined her. "This particular piece of mountain just happens to be situated in such a way that it traps a lot of solar radiation. The heat fools the wildflowers into blooming like this out of season. The magic act will stop, though, when the heavy snowfalls start—which ought to be any day now."

Unable to wait any longer, Kristin tore into the sack lunch Addie had packed, hoping that what was inside would be half as good as her streusel. It became immediately clear that High Country's manager was adept at feeding ravenous skiers. The lunch featured lean roast-beef sandwiches on homemade wheat bread, tart Taos apples to be eaten with chunks of cheddar cheese, chewy oatmeal-pecan cookies, and a thermos of hot spiced tea.

"Bless you, Addie Watkins," Lowrey laughed, holding a thick sandwich aloft in tribute.

After a few minutes, during which they both devoted themselves to uninterrupted eating, Kristin started to ask Lowrey a question. She hesitated over the proper way to address him, discarding Mr. Lowrey as too formal after their morning together and Gray as too informal.

"Grayson—" she began, but before she could ask the question, she was cut off.

"Call me Gray, everyone else at High Country does."

"Does that mean . . ." Kristin was afraid to complete the thought, much less the sentence, that had instantly formed in her astonishingly presumptuous mind. He couldn't possibly have meant what she hoped he had.

"You got the job?" Gray finished it for her. "It most assuredly does. You're a good skier, Kristin. I'd have no qualms about entrusting a class of beginners to your care and instruction. Of course, I'd have to check out your orienteering, first aid, and survival skills a bit more closely before I sent you out to guide any overnighters. But the instructor's job's yours if you want it."

Kristin forced herself to contain her joy at Gray's decision. Though cannons were exploding and bells pealing inside her head, Kristin followed Gray's cool lead and replied with all the nonchalance she could manufacture that she did indeed want the job. She couldn't prevent the happy glow that radiated from her as she spoke the words, a glow that Gray noted with some satisfaction.

"Now, what was that question you were about to ask before I interrupted?" he inquired.

Kristin had to concentrate to remember what it was she was thinking of before making the exhilarating discovery that she had won a winter at High Country! "Oh," she stumbled, "I was going to ask how long High Country had been in operation."

"This will be the start of our ninth season," Gray answered, warming to a subject that was obviously close to his heart. "It's only been in the last four or five years, though, that there's been any sizable interest in cross-country. For most of its existence, I've had to float the lodge with what I made at my downhill place."

Kristin liked the way he referred to an internationally known resort like Powderhorn as his "downhill place."

"I guess that High Country is my favorite. Over the past few years Alpine skiing has turned into a flashy, technology-crazed sport. There's no solace, no chance to be alone with the mountain in downhill anymore, like there was in the beginning. Not like there still is in cross-country."

"I know," Kristin agreed. "I grew up ski touring in Wisconsin. Back then army surplus was in vogue, but it really didn't matter what you wore, because you so rarely saw another human being. Downhill skiing is a fashion parade in comparison." Gray nodded. Feeling that there was far, far more to Gray Lowrey than she had first suspected, Kristin gave in to her growing curiosity about him. "Have you always skied or did you do other sports while you were growing up? Like football." She supplied what she suspected would be the answer to her question.

"Touché." Gray laughed. "I guess I deserved that for making the hasty assumption yesterday that you were looking for work as a cocktail waitress."

Kristin was pleased by the openhanded way he admitted his mistake.

"Yes, as a matter of fact, I did play football," Gray allowed. "For exactly one day. Given my size, which was delivered early," he explained wryly, "it was natural, once I started filling out, that I'd be encouraged to participate in the Great American sport." His tone was derisive. "So I went out for the team in junior high. The tryout consisted of a scrimmage. The coach ordered us all 'not to be babies,' to 'hit 'em hard.' I followed his order and tackled this kid with all I had. When the dust cleared, the kid was sitting in the middle of the field with tears running down his cheeks. I'd dislocated his shoulder." The ironic contempt in Gray's voice gave way to genuine pain at the memory of his having hurt another human.

As if he'd revealed too much of himself, Gray finished with a light, "And that was the beginning *and* the end of my football career. But I believe you started off asking me if I'd always skied. I'll answer that by telling you where I grew up—Kansas."

"Then, I'd guess," Kristin said with mock shrewdness, "you probably didn't."

"No, the powder wasn't too great in the cornfields,"

he joked in return. "And, since cross-country was unheard of there, I wasn't introduced to either Nordic or downhill skiing until a spring break trip I took to the Rockies during my junior year of college."

"What were you studying?"

"Mostly hell-raising and woman-chasing," Gray teased, his grin strikingly white against his dark beard and tanned face. "No, seriously, my major didn't matter, because as soon as I saw these mountains I—" Gray paused, his glance encompassing the soul-stretching panorama before them. "I knew, finally, where I belonged." He finished quietly. "I hung on after break and wangled a job as a lift operator. After a few months of gorging myself on skiing the deep powder, I came to the conclusion that I wanted my own chunk of mountain that I could run my own way. I scouted the area for a couple of years until I found just the right piece of real estate. Fortunately, no one else was too interested in my mountain and I leased it from the Forest Service for a song. After that, the work started. I had to sing and dance my way into the hearts and wallets of a couple dozen investors in order to put in a ski lift—a secondhand T-bar run by a twelve-horsepower diesel engine." Gray smiled at the memory of the dilapidated piece of equipment. "But tourists came, by God, and I got those skiers up the mountain."

Kristin saw the gleam of a visionary in Gray Lowrey, the spark of a man who thrives on turning dreams into reality. Perhaps that was what had prompted him to accept her challenge, to take a day out of what was clearly a very full schedule to give her a chance to make her dream materialize. *And it has materialized*, she thought with exultation.

"And what about yourself?" Gray asked, taking his turn at the questions. "What made you so hell-bent to get the instructor's job? Are you running from a broken love affair?" he theorized teasingly.

Though his show of interest pleased Kristin, she wasn't up to resurrecting the gloomy story of her failed exhibit. She'd come to High Country to file that sad chapter of her life in the past. "Something like that," she answered with deliberate ambiguity.

Though she would never have thought it possible at the meal's beginning, Kristin realized before she was halfway through Addie's lunch that she couldn't eat another bite. With a groan, she sank back against the mountain. The trapped warmth Gray had mentioned was quite evident, pulsing from the ground in waves perfumed with the fragrance of wildflowers. From her vantage point more than twelve thousand feet high, the entire world seemed to sweep out in front of her. The combination of that view, her full stomach, the morning's exertion, the dizzying, wildflower-scented warmth, and the prospect of a winter at High Country created a contentment unlike any Kristin had ever known before. A languorous weariness stole over her.

"I think I could stay here, just like this, forever," she murmured, surprised at how comfortable she felt with her new employer. Gray, while he certainly commanded respect, was not a person Kristin could cast in the role of the stereotypical boss. She suspected that the effort a person like Mr. Pershing extracted from his staff through threats and constant surveillance, Gray could elicit effortlessly, simply by the loyalty he inspired.

Gray, his arms crossed over his knees, gazed out toward the far horizon. "That's Wheeler Peak out there," he said, pointing to New Mexico's highest mountain. "The Native Americans believe that . . ."

But Kristin never learned what the Native Americans believe about Wheeler Peak for, when Gray turned toward her, he ceased speaking. The noonday sun streamed over Kristin, bringing the gold in her hair and eyes to life. It danced over her full lips and lightly freckled nose. It warmed and soothed the long limbs Gray had seen carry her so far and with such lithe grace.

"Your hair and eyes," he mumbled, as if he'd just noticed she had them. "The color is so . . ." Gray hesitated, seeming to consciously discard all the familiar adjectives like *pretty* and *striking*, which Kristin had heard applied to her coloration. Finally, he settled on a markedly uneffusive description. "Unusual," he finished. He reached out a strong, tanned hand and touched the very tail end of her braid, lying on the ground beside him. "An unusual copper color," he said. His voice sounded dry and raspy.

Her scalp tingled from the light tug of Gray toying with her hair. Kristin thought of the contrast between Gray and someone like Dennis Hascomb. In his glib, hyper-articulate way, Dennis had controlled their relationship from the very start. In contrast, Gray seemed almost mutely elemental, like a wild mountain creature drawn to her by the coppery glitter of her hair. Yet Kristin knew that was an illusion. This was Gray's world. He ruled it not just by force of ownership but through his physical mastery of it.

The tingling stopped abruptly, and Gray clenched his hands together, looking off once more into the distance. The sudden gesture confirmed an intuitive awareness that now formed in Kristin's conscious mind: *He wants to touch me*, she thought. She remembered how she had reacted in exactly that way to the sight of Gray's sculptured torso and realized that she might be evoking the same response in him. It gave her a sense of oddly precarious power. Odd because she wanted to know the feel of him beneath her fingers as much as he seemed to want to know her, and precarious because, in the final analysis, she knew that the power on Diablo Peak would always be his.

Kristin felt enclosed within the translucent shell of a fragile moment. She almost dared not breathe for fear of shattering it. Yet she was equally afraid of losing it, allowing it to slip away, never to be reclaimed. Impulse had always been the driving force behind her work and had guided her toward the best decisions of her life. She submitted to it now. Sitting up, she reached out a tentative hand and, with a touch so light as to be nearly imperceptible, laid it upon his upper arm.

Gray jerked around to face her with an almost accusatory expression that melted away at the sight of Kristin's quizzical look. "What is it, Gray?" she asked.

The question precipitated the response Kristin had wanted more than she knew. As Gray slowly rolled toward her, giving her ample opportunity to change her mind and pull her hand away, Kristin felt as though she were on the brink of triggering an avalanche, of deliberately skiing over the top of a slab of snow she knew was about ready to give way. Still she did not take her hand away.

Instead, she slid it up the muscled bounty of his arms and shoulders and down the columns of his back. The sheer size of him was a revelation to Kristin, who had always somehow ended up with men her own size or only slightly larger. Such an abundance of maleness seemed a rampant luxury. The muscles quivered beneath Kristin's touch, as if coming fully awake after a long slumber. With a barely controlled slowness, he leaned toward her.

“This is insane,” Gray groaned at the instant in which they both abandoned themselves to the mutual lunacy. Kristin felt herself being pressed back against the heat of the mountain and then sandwiched between it and the warmth pouring from Gray’s chest. Her lids drooped; she was drugged by the intoxicating odors assailing her. The mingling of the fragrance of the wildflowers and Gray’s own male smell was heady.

He grappled briefly with the zipper at the neck of her turtleneck, opened it, then feasted hungrily on the creamy skin he had exposed. The delicious rasp of his beard against her neck sent tendrils of electric sensation spiraling out from that sensitive spot. Gray looked down at her, his eyes dark, searching, asking yet one more time if she wouldn’t stop him. Kristin trailed her hands up his spine to the tautness at the base of his neck, threaded her fingers through his sun-streaked hair, and, with a slight, gentle pressure, brought his head down. The avalanche had begun to fall.

His breathing accelerated and Kristin could feel the thunder of his heartbeat resonating in her chest to match the racing beat of her own pulse. His lips took possession of hers with an astonishing swiftness, pressing urgent demands against their fullness. Gray had stopped asking permission. He parted her lips, his tongue hungrily exploring the recesses beyond. Kristin’s hands on his cheeks felt the delicious thrusts. In one panther-quick movement, Gray reversed their positions, rolling onto his back and pulling Kristin over on top of him.

For that brief moment in which she was toppled about as easily as if she *had* been caught in an avalanche, Kristin was frightened by the ferocity of the power she had unleashed. Then his hands began to artfully knead her back, neutralizing even the threat of tension. The sun and his skillful massage made Kristin feel as if she were melting, that soon she would be little more than a runny puddle on Grayson Lowrey's chest. As soon as she was reduced to a gelatinous mass, however, the hands began to reenergize her. They descended down her back, over the springy muscles of her buttocks, and onto the backs of her thighs to tantalize the nerve-rich flesh there.

His abdominal muscles hardened beneath her as he lifted up his head, reaching to seek out Kristin's mouth again. He pulled her tighter against the swelling evidence of his desire. Her own arousal was equally obvious in her quickened breath. Gray raked a hand upward, lingering over the dip of her waist, the arch of her rib cage, the thrust of her breasts.

Kristin gasped at the rush of pleasure that flooded her. Even through the thin cotton of the turtleneck, the feel of Gray's hand on her breast, of his thumb teasing her nipple, caused an aching spasm to throb in her very core. He pinned her chin in both his hands and kissed her with a desperate urgency that left her fighting for air. She opened her eyes to gaze at the man who had excited her with a force she had never experienced before.

Feeling her scrutiny, Gray opened his eyes. He had the dazed appearance of a man fighting his way out of a coma. Thinking that the sun was in his eyes, Kristin moved to his side so that he could sit up. But even then there was a narrowing in Gray's eyes that chilled Kristin as he returned her gaze. His nostrils were flared like those of a renegade horse struggling at the end of a captor's lasso. His breathing was irregular. Kristin knew that she too exhibited similar symptoms and was betraying the extent of her arousal.

As the moment lengthened and he made no move to encircle her once more within the enflaming bonds of his arms, Kristin began to wonder what was stopping him. He couldn't be unaware of her need for him. As a brisk wind swept down from the top of Diablo Peak, Kristin yearned for the warmth they had shared. It was clear, however, that the warmth was rapidly dissipating beneath Grayson Lowrey's cold scrutiny of her.

"I'm sorry," he said, his voice even huskier than it normally was.

"Sorry for what?" Kristin demanded.

"I took advantage of my position."

"Gray, you must be joking. There were no advantages taken here. I wanted you to touch me, to kiss me." Kristin shivered as humiliation cooled the fires that had raged within her.

He eyed her as if rechecking his decision. Kristin couldn't guess what he had seen in her face, but, whatever it was, it cemented his decision. He rose to his feet.

"Take my word for it," he said, extending a hand down from his seigneurial height to help her up, "it wouldn't have worked."

Kristin stiffened. The rebuff struck her directly in her already wounded ego. Never before had she dared to show such aggressiveness, to allow her need to surface so plainly; never before had she been devastated by a man's rejection. She had to call upon her already seriously depleted reserves of dignity to rise graciously to her feet and pretend that nothing had happened, because that was obviously what Grayson Lowrey intended to do.

"Don't be offended," he said commandingly.

Kristin gave a derisive snort of laughter. "Perhaps you'd also like to advise me 'not to take it personally.'"

"You have every right to be angry." The ragged edge to his voice warned Kristin of the effort he was making to restrain himself. "I never should have let myself get carried away."

"No, you shouldn't have," she agreed tartly, deliberately tempting the control he was exercising. "Not when you had no intention of, shall we say, following through."

"Whatever conclusions you've come to about me, about us," the desire-deepened voice rumbled on, "they're wrong. You're a very desirable woman, Kristin. I think you know that. I think you also know that I wanted very much to have you. But not . . ." He held up his hands in exasperation, either at his failure or his refusal to say more. "I can't allow myself," he stated with a flat finality.

Kristin tried to imagine what he might have started to say, but no explanation she could formulate would have excused what he'd done. If Kristin had felt that a special bond existed between him and the craggy summits that were his domain, she now saw a positive resemblance as a granite firmness froze his features. At that moment, Kristin felt more alone than she would have had she been all by herself. She knew that the frosty discipline Gray was exercising was directed toward keeping her emotionally at bay. With a stab of regret over what might have been, Kristin bowed to the strength of the rocky facade that had been erected as a barrier against her. She bent over to retrieve her pack. There was a long and precipitous descent ahead; she intended to make it a swift one as well.

Chapter 4

Kristin leaned on her poles, bent over at the waist, trying to recapture her breath. The descent had been even swifter than she'd intended. She'd outdistanced Gray, though she knew that the feat was less a tribute to her skill than to his tact. He'd simply allowed her the time to herself he undoubtedly had realized she needed. The lodge's front door swung open and Addie Watkins stepped out, wiping her hands on a dish towel.

"Saw you coming down from the kitchen window. Lordy God, child, you certainly do burn up a mountain, don't you."

Kristin smiled weakly.

"Is anything wrong?" Addie asked.

Kristin was irritated by her own transparency. She didn't want anyone at High Country to know how Grayson Lowrey had humiliated her. "No, just trying to catch my breath," Kristin lied, exaggerating her strained inhalations.

"Where's Gray?" Addie asked, a hand billing her forehead as she searched the hills. "It's not like him to let a newcomer find her own way down."

"I doubt that he was too far behind me," Kristin answered, hoping to smooth the lines that worry had suddenly creased into Addie's features. She certainly wasn't about to discuss the generous lead Gray had given her so that she could be alone to recover from what had happened, or failed to happen, between them.

A tawny blur burst out of the front door and streaked with a joyous exuberance directly toward Kristin, knocking her into a cushioning snowbank.

"Punkin', you orange monster." Kristin scolded the dog with a laughing fierceness. The retriever lapped melting snowflakes off of her mistress's face by way of welcoming her home.

As Kristin fought her way back to her feet, Addie announced, "Here he comes now." Kristin followed Addie's finger to a dark silhouette chiseling a series of sinuous S-curves into the snow on the steeply pitched mountainside. Kristin had known instinctively that this was how Gray would ski, with a powerful command that would lend to his every motion a sort of controlled grace. From a distance Gray might have been the instrument of a master calligrapher as he painted a fluid, unwavering design onto an endless roll of white rice paper.

Concern dropped from Addie's face like snow sliding off a pitched roof as Gray swept down Diablo Peak. Kristin hurriedly popped the release mechanism on her skis.

"I'd better change out of these wet clothes," she babbled, grabbing for the first excuse that came to mind for effecting a hasty retreat. Kristin was determined not to let the episode on Diablo Peak rob her of the winter of healing she needed so badly. She also realized that, sooner or later, she would have to face her employer. It was just that, at the moment, she definitely preferred that the encounter occur sometime later. She wasn't yet up to confronting the man who had aroused her so intensely, then rejected her such a short time before.

Kristin, with Punkin' at her heels, fled toward the sanctuary of the lodge's dark interior. Puzzlement clouded Addie's face as Kristin brushed past her, but it wasn't until she was inside that Kristin understood what had caused Addie's perplexed expression—she had no clothes to change into and no room in which to undress even if she had brought in a dry outfit.

The memories of many a long winter's night hung in the piñon-scented air of the lodge. Kristin found a remote corner and crumpled into it, feeling the double sting of her aching muscles and pride. She had nowhere to hide.

She couldn't run from Gray, not in his own lodge. She settled into the heavy pine chair and Punkin' draped her large head over Kristin's knee. Mechanically, she patted the dog's head and scratched behind her floppy ear. Soon Punkin's eyes closed into two slits of canine bliss. But Kristin's mind was far away: She was envisioning the inevitable encounter with Gray. The prospect stirred a confusion of emotions running from dread to a reluctantly admitted anticipation.

"I thought we were going to have to send out a search party for you." Addie's twangy voice carried easily into the lodge's cool depths. "Kristin beat you down by ten minutes."

Kristin winced at Addie's unintentional blunder. She braced herself for Gray's angry retort in which he would correct the mistaken impression that his new instructor had bested him on his own mountain.

"She's a fine skier," was all Gray said. "She starts to work for me as soon as I can officially enter her name on the payroll. Get her oriented, will you, Addie? I'm going on up to Powderhorn."

Gray's deep bass voice seemed to fill the air around Kristin. She breathed in the sound of his words and they constricted her chest until she could barely inhale.

"But, Gray," Addie protested, "how are we going to get the lodge ready to open? There's still a lot that needs to be done here and Powderhorn won't be opening for a while yet. You'd planned to stay on here for the rest of the week to supervise all those renovations we talked about."

Kristin's heart sank—Gray was going to the great inconvenience of restructuring his life for the sole purpose of avoiding her.

"You can handle it, Addie." Gray soothed his distraught lodge manager. "I'll send a couple of the boys over from Powderhorn to help you out."

Kristin heard the creak of a ski rack being raised and the clatter of skis as Gray attached his cross-country equipment to the top of his Ford Bronco. "I'll be in touch." Gray's eagerness for escape wasn't hard for Kristin to discern.

"Hold on a minute, mister," Addie demanded, cutting short his getaway. "You've missed a few details, like what room am I supposed to put Kristin up in and what did you hire her to do?"

"Instruct," Gray replied tersely. "And put her in any room you choose; it doesn't matter which one." The clipped brusqueness of Gray's answer, the ease with which he dismissed her, stabbed at Kristin. "On second thought," he continued, "put her in the blue gingham room."

"But that was—"

"I know what it was, Addie." For the first time, a sharp edge sliced through Gray's words. In a gentler tone, he asked, "Help her get settled in, all right?"

"Sure, Gray, whatever you want."

"Thanks, Addie, I can always count on you."

The grind of the Bronco's engine was fading in the distance when Addie entered the lodge. She stared at Kristin for a minute in silence, then finally spoke. "I know something happened today up there on Diablo Peak," she began tentatively. "Gray's as easy to read as a book. I also know that it's none of my business what it was that went on, so I'll just say what I feel like I've got to say, then we'll drop the subject." Addie drew in a deep breath as if steeling herself for the onerous task she'd taken on.

"I've known Grayson Lowrey for almost ten years now. He hired me as a cook, which is all I'd ever been from the day my mother died and I took over feeding the hired hands on my daddy's ranch. Later on, after I left home, I worked off of a chuckwagon, going from ranch to ranch feeding roundup crews. Then I did short-order work at every truck stop between here and Flatonia. Came up to Taos to visit some kinfolk and heard that there was an opening for a cook at High Country. I've never left these mountains since the day I applied for that job." Addie recited her résumé with a blustery directness, sighed, and added, "All that was a long-winded way of saying that I never expected to be anything but a cook.

Figured they'd just bury me with a spatula in my hand and that'd be the end of Addie Watkins." She laughed her easy, country laugh. "But Gray just kept giving me more responsibilities, kept letting me try new things, and didn't care if I wasn't perfect the first time. I finally ended up managing the place."

A kind of surprised pride welled up in Addie's words. Beneath the pride, Kristin sensed the deep loyalty Addie felt to the man who had given her the chance to end her days as something more than a short-order cook at a truck stop.

"He even set up this profit-sharing plan to make me a real part of the operation. Now," Addie went on, solemn again, "he didn't have to do any of that; he could have left me in the kitchen just like all those truck-stop owners and ranchers always did. But he didn't and I'm mighty grateful. I'll tell you flat out, I'd walk over hot coals for Grayson Lowrey." Addie's intensity startled Kristin as she added, "And I'll tell you one other thing: Don't get involved with the man."

If Addie hadn't been taking the delivery of her message so seriously, Kristin might have burst out laughing at the unintended, twisted humor of her warning. "You can rest assured," Kristin promised, "that there is no danger of that happening."

"Good." Addie sighed, visibly uncoiling as the tension she'd built up dissipated. "Just thought it only fair to warn you. Women have a rough time with Gray. Leastwise ones that are romantically involved with him. But enough of my jawing," she concluded. "I'd better show you to your room so you can change into those dry clothes you mentioned."

Kristin was surprised by the size of the corner room that was to be hers. It wasn't hard to figure out why Gray had referred to it as the blue gingham room: The four-poster double bed was covered with a thick, fluffy comforter made of the material, as were the curtains at the window. A woolly sheepskin rug spanned the distance between the bed and the room's own private fireplace. Punkin' promptly settled herself down on it, signaling to Kristin that she too was pleased with their new accommodations.

"It's lovely!" Kristin exclaimed. There was another surprising aspect, though, which she'd also noticed. She fingered the blue-and-white fabric at the window. It was still impregnated with the sizing that had been applied at the factory to stiffen the material on the bolt. At the same time the white checks were ever so slightly yellowed with age. "It almost looks like everything here is brand new but also years old." She looked to Addie for an explanation and saw the older woman flinch involuntarily.

"You'd probably find out sooner or later," she admitted reluctantly. "This was Mrs. Lowrey's room. She only stayed in it a few times, though. Didn't like High Country. Preferred Powderhorn even when Gray was here."

"'Mrs.' Lowrey." Kristin echoed the title, feeling fresh shame burn through her at the discovery that Gray was a married man.

"I should say the *ex*–Mrs. Lowrey," Addie corrected herself. "They've been divorced for some time, though he hasn't allowed anyone into this room before now. . . . Well, if you'll give me the keys to your station wagon, I'll have Eric bring up your luggage and you can get moved in."

As the door closed behind Addie, Kristin forced herself to chase all thoughts of Grayson Lowrey from her mind. She rushed from one high window to the other, reveling in the glorious view each offered. One opened onto the pine and aspen valley sweeping out below the lodge; the other looked directly onto Diablo Peak. Kristin hurriedly left that window and, after discovering a spacious closet, cautiously turned the knob of yet another door. She was delighted to discover that it led into a private bath. A knock brought her to the main door, and she opened it to find a short, sturdily built young man with a headful of shiny black curls clutching one of her suitcases in each stocky hand.

"Hi, I'm Eric Malther. I presume you've already been introduced to your luggage," he quipped with a ready smile as he held up the bags.

"Oh, thanks," Kristin answered, backing away quickly to allow Eric into the room. "Just put them down anywhere."

Relieved of his load, Eric stuck his hand out for a proper introduction. "I assume you're Kristin Jonsson, new instructor."

"Assumption correct," Kristin said, returning his hearty shake.

"I do some instructing, but mostly I guide guests into the more remote or avalanche-prone areas or take them out on overnight trips. So, basically, I'm gone a lot. When I'm around here I'm Mr. Fix-it and Jack-of-all-trades. I guess we all are really. No one is 'just' a guide or 'just' an instructor. We all help out where we're needed. You'll meet my fiancée, Betsy. She's here mostly because I am. She hates being outside in the snow, so she works around the lodge making beds and helping Addie. This is temporary for both of us. Bets is getting her master's in medieval literature, and next fall I'll have to return to the real world and start looking for work as a computer programmer. And, now that you know more about Eric Malther than you ever wanted to," Eric said with an impish grin, "tell me what you do in the real world."

"I was working as a technical artist," Kristin answered, omitting her true ambition. She liked Eric's distinction between this snowy mountain refuge and the "real world." She had failed in that world; here she could pretend her exhibit had never happened.

"Addie told me to tell you that dinner's at six and you'd better bring an appetite," Eric informed her as he headed for the door.

"Thanks," Kristin called out after him as he made his way down the wide staircase. So far, High Country Lodge had exceeded all her expectations. The mountains were magnificent, her accommodations bordered on luxurious, and she'd instantly liked everyone she'd met connected with the lodge. Everyone except . . . The name Grayson Lowrey flashed into Kristin's mind, but her innate honesty forced her to censor it out. Though it galled her to have to admit it, she was far from disliking the man, in spite of his brutal rejection.

A sudden weariness attacked Kristin and she yielded to the temptation the feathery comforter offered. Sunk into its cushioning depths, Kristin replayed the entire episode. Again she felt the hard strength of Gray's back beneath her fingers, the intoxicating force of his lips upon hers, the wind's chill as he turned from her. One part of her yearned to castigate Grayson Lowrey as an insensitive, callous boor—and something of a tease to boot. But her infuriating honesty prevailed, forcing her to rip the blinders of wounded pride away and examine the incident from Gray's perspective.

Kristin winced as she saw how her behavior might have appeared to Gray and realized that she had foolishly overplayed her hand, pushing her new employer toward an intimacy that he had neither sought nor desired. She knew why he had initially responded to her—any man would have, simply to prove his virility. But then he had stopped. Not flinching from the brutal self-examination, Kristin went on to enumerate some possible explanations for the cooling of Gray's ardor. The most immediate one was suggested by her room—the blue gingham room—a virtual shrine to a former wife. Kristin decided that it wouldn't be too far-fetched to assume that Gray was still emotionally tethered to his former wife.

Or perhaps he was trying to protect a more current involvement? Maybe one of the Powderhorn cocktail waitresses that he'd initially assumed she wanted to become. Then again, Kristin theorized, she might have been expecting something that Mr. Grayson Lowrey simply didn't have to offer—warmth. His rebuff might have been an act of kindness, saving her from his emotional bankruptcy.

There was one last alternative that Kristin's ruthlessly truthful mind would not allow her to ignore—perhaps Grayson Lowrey had simply not found her attractive. That one stung, but in the same way that iodine on a cut stings as it disinfects the wound. Facing up to the worst somehow had a cleansing effect on Kristin, and she sat back up, feeling surprisingly refreshed. She was proud of herself for tackling head-on the team of mental hobgoblins that had sprung up that afternoon before they'd had the opportunity to multiply into a small army and destroy her winter in the Sangre de Cristos.

A quick shower buoyed her up as much as the resolution she made with herself—her future encounters with Gray would offer no opportunity for any further awkwardness.

Dinner turned out to be an endless parade of edibles that testified to the massive caloric needs imposed by cold weather and vigorous exercise. Addie gave a delighted chuckle in response to Kristin's open-eyed wonder at the bounteous table surrounded by ruddy sun- and wind-burned faces.

"This will be one of my last chances to cook," Addie explained. "During the season I'm too busy to get into the kitchen much. Decided you needed a real Welcome to High Country feast to get you fattened up some if you're going to last the winter here." The faces around the loaded table smiled approbation and welcome. Kristin took a seat beside Eric. A delicately featured young woman on his other side leaned over him. "Hello," she said in a wispy voice. "I'm Betsy."

Kristin returned the introduction, noting that Eric and his fiancée, with their twin sets of curly, dark hair, looked like brother and sister: a hearty, outdoors brother and his ethereal, academic sister. A flurry of introductions followed as Kristin met the burly lift operators and members of the crews that cleared trails and kept them maintained.

Greetings were followed by round after round of steaming bowls and platters being passed to and fro in front of Kristin. She sank gratefully into the friendly tumult, cheered by the rattle of silverware against heaping plates and voices raised in good-humored conversation. She was neither ignored nor paid undue attention. Rather, Kristin felt herself an immediate part of the group, accepted for just what she was or would be at High Country. Deep within her she experienced a sense of ease that she hadn't known for a long time, almost as if the healing she had sought had begun on the spot. A sliver of worry disturbed her calm, however. How would she fare when the time came for her to take on a class completely alone? She decided to put aside that concern for the time being and dug her fork into the cheesy broccoli casserole on one edge of her plate.

The next few days were lost in a scurrying bustle of cleaning and repair work as Kristin labored beside the rest of the High Country staff and the extra men sent over from Powderhorn to ready the lodge for the start of the season. Their efforts proved to be well-timed because, just as the last window was washed and the last fireplace put in working order, ominous gray clouds began churning up over the valley, sending shrill winds whistling down the canyons, shrieking their message to man and beast alike—winter was coming. After issuing that warning, the skies opened up and inch upon inch of the dry, powdery snow that is the skier's dream sifted down, blanketing the mountains and the freshly carved trails in fluffy white.

The first wave of cross-country skiers followed the snowplows clearing the roads up the mountain to High Country. Kristin discovered just how true Eric's words were as she, along with everyone else at the lodge, pitched in and helped wherever and whenever she was needed. That first week she showed guests to their rooms, carried in luggage, and fetched clean towels. Among the guests was a group of students from the University of New Mexico who'd driven up from Albuquerque with their mandatory sponsor in a dilapidated van. There was also a contingent of artists and craftspeople from Santa Fe and an assortment of young professional couples and their children. Kristin even met a balloon pilot and his family, his name and face familiar to her from countless newspaper and magazine articles.

What she noticed about all of them, rich and poor, famous and unknown alike, was how they were affected by High Country Lodge. They all arrived tense and a bit cranky from the strain of a long drive up treacherous, ice-slicked mountain roads. But, after a few short hours, the tension dissolved like a morning fog as the same ease that she herself had discovered at the lodge seemed to pervade everyone. Perhaps it was the homelike quality of the lodge, or maybe it was the spell woven by the majesty of the Sangre de Cristos looming above them. Whichever it was, Kristin rarely had the feeling that she was an employee, a hireling. Guests too seemed to become a part of the lodge, finding far more than simple shelter within its thick pine walls.

Kristin awoke the morning she was to teach her first class and looked down from her second-story window onto a world of white sunshine. She silently thanked the mountain gods for a day that made the new-fallen snow glitter with an eye-piercing brilliance. Beginners always got a psychological boost from the radiance of a clear day; it made snow-covered mountains seem a bit less foreboding.

"Beginners' class," Kristin called out as she stood in front of the main hall's fireplace. With the skis they'd just acquired at the rental shop rattling in their hands, a crowd of first-time tourers converged on Kristin. She quickly estimated that they ranged in age from a pretty preteen blonde—the daughter of a pair of Sante Fe lawyers—to the grandfatherly university professor who'd come up as the sponsor of a vanload of students. In between were the wives, husbands, children, and sweethearts of the more advanced skiers who had left earlier that morning with Eric for a more rugged backcountry outing.

Kristin surveyed the eager faces that turned to her with that precise combination of trust and expectancy bestowed upon teachers. She drew in a deep, steadying breath and prayed that she wouldn't disappoint her students. "Hi, I'm Kristin Jonsson. That's two *s*'s and no *h*, and, before this day is over, I guarantee that each and every one of you will be able to paddle through that world of snow out there just like it was an ocean of feathers." She pumped her first words full of confidence and the carefully cultivated optimism that she could transfer her love of the snowy outdoors to the first class for which she was entirely responsible.

Kristin watched the response to her promise. Most of the faces lighted up, infatuated with the idea of skimming over an "ocean of feathers," and Kristin silently blessed whatever benevolent spirit had put the fortuitous phrase into her brain. Only the professorial gentleman displayed any hint of antagonism. He shook his head as if the idea were preposterous, and Kristin made a special note to see to it that he received extra attention. She had no intention of reneging on her promise.

"And now I'd like to introduce my assistant, Punkin'." At the sound of her name, the dog bounded up from her spot in front of the fireplace and pranced at Kristin's side. All hint of first-day jitters evaporated at the appearance of the galumphing canine, and Kristin knew the dog would fulfill her function of providing comic relief.

"Before we get started, let me give you a brief history of the sport. Cross-country skiing, or ski touring, started in Scandinavia over four thousand years ago. It was imported to this country by Scandinavian immigrants in the early 1800s. By the time of the 1849 gold rush, miners were using a heavy, unwieldy ancestor of today's lighter, skinnier ski to transport themselves over the High Sierras. From the Second World War on, skiing in America has come to mean the speedy thrills of the downhill variety. It is only quite recently that skiers have left the packed downhill trails and ventured into the wilds accessible only on these funny kinds of skis you all are holding right now. Cost has been one reason for ski touring's increasing popularity; another is that it's easy to learn. If you can walk, you can ski cross-country. Are you all ready to give it a try?"

A ragtag chorus of affirmatives went up, joined in by everyone except the disgruntled professor. Kristin led her band out to the pasture, a level clearing behind the lodge that she'd designated as her classroom. A cheek-tingling breeze was kicking up spindrifts of snow that whirled in the sunlight like a granulated prism. After she had ascertained that everyone had been outfitted with beginners' non-wax skis, she had them all buckle them onto their boots. To help her students adjust to having six-foot-long extensions strapped on their feet, Kristin led them in a series of exercises in sliding the unwieldy skis back and forth. Next she led them around the track that had been grooved into the large pasture. Poles were added then.

"This is called the 'outhouse crouch,'" Kristin announced as she adopted the bent-knees posture of the cross-country skier leaning forward onto his poles. "Try a few steps," she urged her class.

"I feel like Groucho Marx duckwalking across a stage," complained the increasingly cranky professor. But Kristin refused to let his peevishness infect either her or her class. She burst into laughter. The professor gave her a startled glance; he was obviously unused to being laughed at.

"That's a wonderful description," she gushed. "I hope you don't mind if I plagiarize it for future classes. That's exactly what tourers look like."

Another older man flicked an imaginary cigar in the professor's direction and mimicked Groucho Marx. "Say the secret *woid*," he said, jerking his eyebrows à la Groucho, "and win an all-expense paid trip to Antarctica." The class laughed at the imitation and the reference to the chilly weather. The professor, sensing that the class was laughing with him, not at him, even managed a frosty smile. Kristin was pleased to see that his next step was made with far more enthusiasm than his previous ones had been.

"Okay," Kristin asserted, "it's just like roller-skating: step, glide, step, glide. As you're kicking off with your right leg, your left hand should be in front of you, reaching out to stab the snow and push off. Left leg, right hand. Right leg, left hand." Kristin called out the rhythms like a bandmaster determining the tempo at which dancers would twirl around him. The first fumbling steps are the hardest, and the class was more than ready when Kristin announced an early lunch break. Fortified by a typically abundant High Country meal, most everyone felt ready to attack the mountain again.

After a short review, Kristin stood in the middle of the pasture and had her students circle around her. When she was satisfied that all her students, even the professor, had mastered the basic motions, she guided them away from the level pasture toward a gently sloping trail. She felt as if she were bestowing a priceless gift upon them as she led her class into a world of winter most of them had never before experienced.

Like a mother duck with a string of slightly awkward ducklings behind her, they struggled up a snow-gullied canyon. Punkin' filled her role as assistant with a frisky exuberance, running back and forth from Kristin's side to the very end of the line as if to encourage the last straggler and check on everyone in general. By diverting them from the task of controlling the skinny skis, Punkin' actually helped Kristin's students to improve their technique by allowing it to become an automatic response.

A teenaged boy was the first to sail past Kristin with a form that she was sure could make him into a Nordic racer if he cared to pursue the sport. Kristin glanced back, pleased to see that most of her students had relaxed enough to let their bodies flow into the gliding motions. Though she doubted he would ever make a racer, even the professor seemed to be enjoying himself, and enjoyment was her primary goal.

Noses were running, cheeks were red, and a few backsides were wet from unexpected encounters with snowbanks by the time the first lesson was over. But Kristin had made good her boast: Every member of her first class was cross-country skiing by the day's end.

There was a shared feeling of accomplishment and the sense of camaraderie that comes from having been part of a group that has met and overcome a challenge as the skiers gathered in the lodge. Steaming mugs of spiced tea appeared as the class collapsed in front of the roaring fire. The scene Kristin had imagined the first time she'd entered the main hall came to life beneath the room's vaulted ceiling as the bubbling music of convivial conversation filled the air. In the middle of the cheery hubbub, the professor rose to his feet and, in his best lecture-hall manner, tapped his teaspoon against a glass. The crowd fell silent. The professor cleared his throat.

"I should like to propose a toast," he affirmed, holding his glass aloft, "to our instructor, who did indeed teach us, even an old, ungainly doubting Thomas like myself, to float on that damned ocean of feathers out there."

"Hear, hear!" came the response, followed by a round of applause that brought a sudden burst of heat flaming in Kristin's cheeks.

"And," the professor continued, holding up a practiced hand for attention, "to her most able assistant, Pun-kin'." Everyone laughed as the object of this latest salvo of praise stuck her black nose perkily into the air as if she understood precisely what had been said and was only too happy to accept the kudos due her.

Now that she had successfully completed her first teaching assignment, Kristin felt the glow of absolute contentment. An untarnished pleasure warmed her from within as she thought of how perfectly everything had worked out for her. Somewhere in the distance a phone rang, but its jangle was barely audible in the chattering crowd. Kristin ignored it; she was already looking forward to the new visitors that the Thanksgiving holidays would bring later on in the week. She couldn't imagine anything that could upset her emotional equilibrium at the moment.

"Kristin." A low voice beckoned her. She turned to

find Addie gesturing to her. Kristin left the amiable company and went to Addie, who was standing off by herself near the reception desk, her hand still on the phone receiver she had just hung up. "I guess it's only fair that I warn you, Gray just called to say that he and his daughter will be staying with us for the Thanksgiving holidays."

Chapter 5

G*ray? Here?" Kristin swallowed Addie's* words, feeling the emotional tranquility she'd been basking in only a moment before shatter.

Addie nodded confirmation. "That was him on the phone just now. He always spends any time he can here at the lodge when his daughter is on vacation from her school in Santa Fe. The homey atmosphere is better for her than a fancy resort like Powderhorn, with everyone coming and going."

"How old is his daughter?" Kristin asked, wanting to know much more.

"Eight," Addie answered. Then, sensing Kristin's restrained curiosity, she added, "Her name is Laurie and she's a very special child, if you know what I mean."

Kristin assumed from the adoring gleam in Addie's eyes that the grandmotherly woman was referring to the maternal interest she'd taken in a child she must have known since the day of her birth.

"I suppose it would make sense for Gray to have tried to find another mother for his child?" Kristin fished gingerly for the information which, in spite of herself, she hungered for. She rationalized her inquiry by telling herself that she was simply testing out the theories she'd formulated for why Gray had rejected her.

"I suppose it would," Addie concurred, "but, as I told you earlier, women don't fare too well with the boss, least not romantically. There hasn't been anyone he's even let come close to replacing Jan—that's his ex—since she left four years ago."

So, Kristin deduced, there was no current love interest in Grayson Lowrey's life. One theory down, three to go.

The days, filled with lessons and an assortment of chores, passed quickly. Before she'd had time to fully prepare herself for the encounter, Kristin awoke Thursday morning to the classic aroma of a turkey roasting and to the unmistakable sound of Gray's Bronco creaking to a halt outside the lodge. The floor was chilly against her bare feet as Kristin bolted out of bed and raced to the window for a glimpse of Gray and his daughter.

Kristin was stunned by the effect that seeing Gray again had upon her. It was as if a disturbing dream that she'd tried to suppress had returned to her conscious memory unbidden and with all the power of the night still intact. Just the sight of his towering figure triggered within her a tactile remembrance of the feel of that tall, muscular body against hers. A remembered whiff of the Alpine wildflowers that blossom only at the distant heights above timberline disoriented her thinking even further. She dragged her scrutiny away from her employer and humiliator to study his daughter, who was sliding off the high seat toward the bank of snow that waited to receive her like a footman's stool.

She was wearing powder-blue corduroy pants and a pink nylon parka with a fuzzy collar. In her hand she proudly clutched several crayon drawings and a finger painting done in orange and purple. One glance at the little girl's wide-set, almond-shaped eyes told Kristin why Addie had called Laurie a "special child"—she had Down syndrome.

Two other qualities about the little girl were also evident even from a height of two stories. The first was apparent to Kristin as Laurie bent down to retrieve the dramatic finger painting that she'd dropped in the snow. She held it up, laughing, her head cocked to one side, as if a terribly funny joke had just been played on her—the child was blessed with the sunniest of natures. Then, when Gray scooped her up in his arms and whirled her around in a joyously demented jig through the sparkling snow, Kristin discerned the second quality—Laurie had a father who loved her deeply.

Seeing the two of them together, watching the way Gray gently tugged the tiny knit cap down on Laurie's wispy brown hair, the way he tenderly wiped her nose, smashed yet another of Kristin's theories about what had happened on Diablo Peak—the one about Gray not having any warmth to share. It was quite evident from the way he cared for his daughter that Gray had an abundance of loving warmth to share if he so desired.

That left Kristin with the two least palatable and most far-reaching of her four theories—Gray either was still emotionally tied to Laurie's mother or he simply had not found Kristin attractive. Kristin chided whatever rebellious part of her it was that kept responding so forcefully to a man with whom there could be no future. She was wondering if she could plead sick and hide out in her room until Gray and his daughter left when Punkin's whimpering caught her attention.

"I guess I can forget *that* plan, eh, girl," Kristin commented, as if she'd discussed the strategy with the dog. "No matter what I do, you're going to need to go downstairs." Kristin decided she needed a bit of confidence fortification, so she pulled on a sleek, one-piece Prussian-blue jumpsuit with a scoop neck over a pewter-colored turtleneck. Perhaps because she had raced in the outfit, topped with a parka of the same stretch material, it always made her feel slightly less vulnerable. Punkin' didn't need any prompting to make the familiar trip downstairs.

Kristin sighed with relief as she successfully maneuvered her way through the main hall and made it outside without running into Gray. At the side of the lodge, playing in the sunny pasture where she always gave her lessons, Kristin found Laurie rolling a ball of snow.

"I'm building a snowman," the little girl announced. Her words were slightly muffled by a tongue a bit too large for her delicate mouth. Still, Kristin had no difficulty understanding either what she'd said or the exuberance behind the statement. "Wanna help me? We can make it a snow girl if you want."

"That's a great idea," Kristin replied, charmed by Laurie's straightforward friendliness. "My name is Kristin," she said, starting to roll another ball of snow across the pasture.

"Mine's Laurie. What's his name?" She touched a tentative mittened finger to Punkin's head. The dog was busily sniffing the powder-blue corduroys.

"She's a girl too," Kristin explained, "and her name is Punkin'."

"Punkin'?" At the sound of her name, Punkin' halted her olfactory investigation and licked the little face near to hers. A look of astonishment followed the lick across Laurie's face and Kristin realized that at the child's school in Santa Fe, she probably hadn't been exposed to many dogs.

"That was a doggie kiss." Kristin quickly interpreted the gesture.

Laurie's astonishment, which was on the verge of dissolving into fear, took a hundred-and-eighty-degree turn and headed straight for delight. Her tilted eyes creased into parabolas of merriment above her rosy cheeks. "A doggie never kissed me before," she exclaimed, patting Punkin's furry head with friendly enthusiasm. "Hey"—she stopped suddenly, looking from the dog to Kristin—"you both have the same color of hair. Just like me and my dad."

Kristin could not stop her amusement at the child's unlikely equation.

"You have a nice laugh."

Kristin whirled around and found herself standing face to chest with Grayson Lowrey. He was carrying some broken skis and old poles.

"Here are the things for the snowman, Button," he told Laurie. One look at the little girl's cutely rounded nub of a nose told Kristin how she'd come by the Button nickname.

"It's going to be a snow girl now," she corrected her father.

Kristin listened to the exchange, her ears numbed by the sudden rush of her pulse. She'd rehearsed a dozen cleverly cutting lines that she'd intended to throw out when she encountered Gray again, but every one of them had vanished.

Gray drove the skis and poles into the snow to wait until Laurie's creation was completed, then he advanced toward Kristin. "Addie tells me you're doing great things with the beginners' classes."

"I try." Kristin could have bit her tongue for forming such a trite response.

"Well, I certainly appreciate your efforts." Gray's comment rang with genuineness.

"Keeps the paying customers happy, right?" Kristin barely recognized her own voice, overlaid as it was by a veneer of snideness. Gray flinched as if the snippy retort had caused him mild, yet real, physical pain.

For the next few seconds they were both silent, both pretending to be absorbed in piling snow together for Laurie's snow girl. Yet each was locked into thoughts of the other. Gray watched as Kristin fit a broken ski beneath his daughter's frozen playmate. Her auburn hair cascaded down her back, making a fiery contrast against the midnight darkness of her jumpsuit. Against his will, his eyes traced the shape of the curves that the stretch material laid bare to his examination. They were as he'd remembered them. He followed the tantalizing line from the thrust of Kristin's breasts, to the plunging tuck of her waist, then back again to the swell of her hips.

It was a form every bit as arousing now as it had been on Diablo Peak. His memory hadn't betrayed him; she was an exceptionally desirable woman. His memory, however, had needed shoring up on one point, and the provocative jumpsuit provided exactly the reminder he needed—Kristin had to be more than slightly aware of her attractiveness to display it so boldly.

With a strength that had been four long years in the building, he reined in his appraisal and reconfirmed the judgment he had reached on Diablo Peak. He had been right then and would stick by the wisdom of that initial assessment, no matter what the cost.

Kristin turned toward Gray just in time to see his gaze cool from warm longing to a frozen determination as chilly as his original rebuff had been. He gestured her toward him. Kristin stood and walked to where he waited out of Laurie's earshot.

"Along with her other, more obvious problems," he said stiffly, "my daughter has a congenital heart defect, so she really shouldn't be playing this vigorously."

Gray's whispered message, along with his coldness in delivering it, left Kristin feeling vaguely guilty, as if she'd enticed the child into deliberately overstraining herself.

"I'm sorry," she muttered, "I didn't know." She was shaken by Gray's silence and disapproving glance. "I had better be going. I have a class to teach."

"Yes," Gray agreed, weighting his words with a heavy

undertone of meaning, "that probably would be for the best."

Kristin pasted a sickly grin on her face as she returned Laurie's cheery wave. Gray rushed to his daughter's side and quickly turned the little girl away from Kristin's departing figure, as if he wanted to wipe her image from Laurie's mind as thoroughly as he seemed to be wiping it from his own.

Kristin took no joy in her lesson that day, nor could she keep herself from wondering about Gray's reaction to her. What had she done? she wondered. Apparently she had unwittingly committed some grievous offense that she couldn't even begin to guess at. She briefly considered skipping Addie's Thanksgiving feast. Fortunately, the resilience that had seen her through the devastation of her first photo exhibit surfaced. Feeling the healthy smoldering of anger begin to thaw out her gumption, she vowed that if she offended Grayson Lowrey so horribly, *he* could exile himself to some remote corner of the lodge. *She* fully intended to savor every bite of Addie's meal.

"More dressing, Kristin?" Betsy asked, extending a platter of the sage-flavored dish toward her.

Kristin groaned out a refusal. She had more than lived up to her intentions. She glanced around at the tables full of sunburned guests and at the other more familiar faces, those she'd become so fond of in such a short time—Addie, Eric, Betsy, even Laurie had staked a claim on her affections from the first. How perfect sharing this special evening with them would have been without the brooding presence of Grayson Lowrey. Sitting at the head of the table, he had studied her all through the meal, almost as if he were searching her for a missing piece of a puzzle. Kristin had squirmed under his relentless gaze through turkey and dressing. Now, finding herself playing with a piece of pumpkin pie because she was too nervous to eat it, Kristin decided that this silly charade had gone on long enough. If Mr. Grayson Lowrey had something to say to her, he could good and well say it and have it done with. She would have no more of feeling like a specimen on a microscope slide.

To cap the holiday, brandy and coffee were served by the fire. Mustering her courage and poise, Kristin found the dark corner Gray had retreated to and made her request in as neutral a tone as she could counterfeit. "May I have a word with you?"

For a fraction of a second she'd caught him off guard, and a startled elation animated his somber features. It was swiftly sealed off, however, barricaded behind a grim facade. "Certainly," he answered, solemn as the lord of a dank, drafty medieval castle.

"In private." Kristin qualified her request.

After checking to make sure that Laurie was the center of a doting crowd, Gray led the way to his office.

The instant the door was shut behind them, Kristin, like an overheated teakettle, began venting her frustrations. "Look," she started off squarely, "I don't know what it is that I've done to offend you, but I'd like to get it out in the open. You've been stalking me all day long and I'm about fed up with it. I don't care if you thought I was too forward on Diablo Peak, or if you're scared I'm going to attack you again, or if you're carrying a torch for your wife, or what the cause is; you can still treat me with the courtesy you'd afford any other member of your staff." A quaver took her by surprise, making her voice wobble on the last three words, and Kristin felt a great, embarrassing lump gather in her throat. Worse still, a stinging in her eyes warned her that her head-on approach was about to collapse entirely beneath a watery deluge. She turned away, wanting nothing more than to flee.

But a pair of strong hands interrupted her flight toward the door and cradled her shoulders until they'd stopped trembling. Then, with painstaking gentleness, they turned her around.

Through a blurry film of tears she was trying desperately not to shed, Kristin saw again the heartbreakingly vulnerable face of the man who had quit football as a boy because he had inadvertently injured another person.

"Kristin." Her name on his lips had the magic of a revelation. "I'm sorry. I had no idea that I'd hurt you."

"What did you think?" she snapped, more angry with

herself for her ridiculous display of emotions than she was with him. "That rejecting me on Diablo Peak then snubbing me all day today would be my idea of high flattery?"

"No, of course not." His voice was low and soothing. Kristin could imagine him using the same tone with Laurie when she came to him with a scraped knee. "I just never dreamed that anything I could do or say to you would have much of an impact. You're such an attractive woman."

A perplexed expression carried Kristin's instantaneous reaction to Gray's puzzling statement. "What on earth do looks have to do with how badly someone's feelings can be hurt?"

Gray threw up his hands in a gesture of futility and resignation. He shook his head. "I don't know, Kristin; it's just a relationship I've observed a few times. Forget it. All I meant to say was, I'm truly sorry."

There was no mistaking the contrition in Gray's eyes, which had melted from a frosty brown to a softness more reminiscent of spring pansies. "You're not an easy person to figure out, Gray. One moment you seem as approachable as Punkin', then the next you're as aloof as the Abominable Snowman."

"You're right," Gray responded without further elaboration. He smoothed some stray copper hairs away from Kristin's face and tucked them in behind her ears. It was such an unutterably tender gesture that Kristin felt every bit of animosity she'd been harboring against this enigmatic man evaporate.

Gray, watching her enmity disappear, was awestruck by the young beauty of the face turned up toward his. Freed of their burden of resentment, Kristin's eyes now sparkled with tears that would, thankfully, go unshed. The damning assessment he had made of the woman before him now seemed only a dim echo of a long-forgotten vow. A vow he hungered to break. The creak of the floorboards as Gray took one measured step forward might just as well have been the sound of two sets of carefully constructed defenses being thrown away.

Kristin felt locked within the force field that swirled about Gray. As he approached her, she was imprisoned within it, a captive of the raw virility of his spirit. It surrounded her. She was walled in, trapped by the rangy body she ached to touch, by its arousing, male smell, its questing strength. Every cell within her seemed alerted to Gray's nearness as her pulse accelerated feverishly.

Then his mouth was upon hers and she was suffused by the force of their mutual desire. Guided only by that desire, Kristin's hands threaded through Gray's silver-peppered beard. Its silky wiriness brought her sensitive palms to tingling life. Through those charged surfaces she felt his driving mouth seek out and explore her own. She yielded thoughtlessly to the thirsting exploration, and Gray's tongue plunged recklessly deep into the warm recesses where her own tongue waited to twine with it in an abandoned dance of sinuous discovery. Her hands tunneled farther back toward the dark thatch of hair that covered Gray's leonine head. Like the most shameless of wantons, Kristin bowed to the compulsion to draw Gray even closer to her. She tugged his head downward and tasted still more deeply of the bone-melting kiss that was so skillfully unraveling the fibers of her resistance.

The sensation of being wrapped within an embrace of warm steel, his lips never leaving hers, was indescribable. Gray reached out a long arm and flicked off the overhead light. They were cloaked in a velvety darkness, the only light coming from a pile of slow-burning embers in the fireplace. Gray guided Kristin to the wide couch and settled her on its supple leather. Like the full sunlight that had bathed Kristin in its radiance on Diablo Peak, the flicker of a fire seemed to wrap her within an enchantment of loveliness.

"My beauty." The words, torn from his throat, were raspy with a wanting he could suppress no more than he could have forbidden the sun to rise.

His face above hers was also illuminated by the fire's blaze. The flames etched the hard lines of his cheeks, brows, and nose while the rest fell away in dark shadows. He kneeled beside her as the jumpsuit she wore fell open with one pull of a long zipper. Hoisting her up to remove the turtleneck, he strafed the creamy mounds of her exposed breasts with his gaze. She trembled as his hand slid over the contours of her waist and undulated upward. His eyes were on hers as his hand closed over the rounded fullness of her breast and he saw her lids flutter closed as his thumb found the stiffened center.

"You're magnificent," he whispered, the words themselves a caress against her ear. "A truly magnificent beauty."

Even as his hands and mouth urged her body on toward a kaleidoscopic realm of sensation, his words suddenly rang an unwanted alarm in her besotted brain. More precisely, it was his tone as he paid homage, for the second time, to her beauty. The words sounded as if they'd been wrung out of him, sounded like those of a tortured man abandoning his true beliefs in order to stop the torment, to find surcease from his pain, if only for a moment.

The disturbance of thought of any kind was erased by the luxurious bristling of Gray's beard tracing a thousand tingling trails down her neck. The journey paused as Gray lapped at the tautened centers of Kristin's breasts, then continued downward. Spirals of quivering awareness were awakened all along her rib cage, the gentle concavity of her stomach. And still the journey continued until the springy hair of his beard, which had dusted her body with sensation, was pressed against her own most intimate growth. Sliding an arm beneath her buttocks, he cupped her to him more fully.

Kristin gasped as his tongue parted her and penetrated to the very core of her pleasure. A liquid silver thrill knifed through her, leaving tendrils of a slower-blooming delight unfolding in its wake. Gently at first, then with an ever-growing insistence, he urged her toward the pinnacle. Under his masterful coaxing, Kristin responded, submitting to the relentless demands of a passion that had been, until this moment, foreign to her. Every nerve in her body seemed to reverberate with an unbearably exquisite overload of sensation, and still Gray went on pleasuring her to a degree she hadn't known possible. Finally, like the brief night blossoming of an exotically rare flower, Gray drew Kristin to a shuddering paroxysm of fulfillment.

Afterward, she needed his arms around her more than ever. She tasted herself in his kiss and felt Gray's still-building excitement begin to rekindle her own. It took several loud knocks on the door before either of them realized that there was someone there. But Gray didn't begin to tear away from her until the thin, hesitant voice called out, "Daddy, are you in there? It's dark up here."

As Gray jerked away from her, Kristin saw his face clearly in the firelight. He had the look of a man coming painfully to his senses. Again she thought of the tortured man renouncing his true beliefs. Now, the instant he was off the rack, he was returning to what he thought right and true. Gray gazed at her almost as if trying to remember who she was. Pierced by an awareness of her nakedness, Kristin scurried to dress herself. Gray went to the door, switching on the harsh overhead light on his way.

He slivered the door open. "I'm here, Laurie," he murmured. "Why don't you go on downstairs for one minute and I'll be right with you? Okay?"

Kristin couldn't make out the little girl's muffled reply, just Gray's firm response. "I promise. Now, scoot." He stood unmoving at the door, his head bent, his back to Kristin, for several long moments before he turned back around. As he did, Kristin tried to read his expression. Tried and failed. All she could discern with certainty was that the heat of a few moments before had been irrevocably iced over.

"Kristin, I . . ." he began feebly, but let his words trail off into a miserable silence. "Forgive me. I never should have allowed what just happened."

"Allowed?" Kristin's astonishment came out as a weak echo of incredulity.

"It wasn't right. Wasn't fair. Not to you, not to me, not to Laurie."

"Laurie? What are you talking about, Gray?"

"I don't want to go into it now, Kristin. Please, just trust me. I have to leave you now. It's for the best. It would have been better if we'd never been alone together, but as it is, I have to leave."

Only the deep, pitiless regret that Kristin heard searing Gray's words kept her anger at bay. Though she may have been humiliated once more, her feelings hurt again, Gray was in much greater pain. His suffering was just as obvious as it was inexplicable. The hurt and bewilderment riddling Kristin were plainly apparent on her face.

"Please, Kristin," Gray begged again. "There's only one thing that's important for you to understand about what's happened between us. I wanted you; God help me, I still want you as I've never wanted another woman in my life. You'll just have to believe that and believe that what I'm doing will be best for all of us." In the silence that followed, his eyes pleaded with her to accept his judgment. Kristin found she could no more resist them than she could the persuasive skill of his lovemaking.

"I believe you, Gray," she whispered as he pulled her to his chest in a final embrace. "I believe you, but I don't understand you." As though her words had released him from a dreaded and ancient curse, Gray left as soon as they were spoken.

For a long time, Kristin sat huddled on the couch watching the embers die away to a dull glow and trying not to think, not to grate for the thousandth time at reasons why. She heard the crunch of Gray's boots on the snow as he strode toward the Bronco. She heard Laurie's voice pipe out in the mountain stillness. "But, Daddy, why are we leaving? We were supposed to stay here for my vacation. Why can't I at least say good-bye to Kristin, Daddy? She helped me build the snow girl. She'll think I don't like her." There was no reply from Gray to overhear, just the decisive slam of a car door and the fading whine of an engine as the vehicle disappeared down a long, dark road.

Chapter 6

T*he winter that year was* an unusually severe one and, in the weeks that followed Thanksgiving, Kristin more often than not awoke to find the sky curdled with gray clouds and a veil of snow pulled around the valley. When the snowfall became so thick and heavy that not even the heartiest of a very hearty breed—the cross-country skier—dared try the hairpin switchbacks that led to the High Country Lodge, a sort of hibernation settled over the staff. Betsy, like a lady-in-waiting out of the medieval literature she studied, turned to one of her endless knitting projects. Eric, for all his high-tech computer knowledge, whiled away the long empty hours carving a chess set with each piece made to resemble a wizened gnome. When heavy weather prevented guests from reaching the lodge, Addie would closet herself in the upstairs office and pore over the bookwork that she was perpetually trying to catch up on.

After exhausting the available reading material, which leaned heavily toward old copies of *Reader's Digest*, Kristin found her vacant hours being devoured by the gloomy thoughts she'd come north to avoid. Besides dwelling on her photo exhibit, however, she now had Grayson Lowrey to add to the list of defeats her unoccupied mind could mull over. Seeking to divert herself, Kristin dragged her suitcase out from under the four-poster bed and dug into it, unearthing her precious non-digital camera and lenses.

She'd planned on merely cleaning the lenses and "exercising the shutters"—snapping off a few shots on the unloaded camera to ensure that the shutter was kept in good working order. But holding the finely wrought equipment in her hand undammed the flood of memories she'd been keeping walled up. Alone among the other art students, she'd been drawn to the beauties and rigors of working with film instead of pixels. With the barrel of a lens cradled in the palm of her hand, she felt again the electric thrill that always shot through her when she'd captured a fresh image. But it was still too soon, too soon to reexperience any of the feelings associated with photography. Perhaps if things had worked out differently with Gray, she mused, she might not have still felt so diffident. *But they hadn't*, she reminded herself with a wounding savagery as she stuffed the camera and lenses back into the suitcase and shoved it under the bed. It was too soon to try again. *It may always be too soon.*

She ripped her parka from the peg where it hung on the back of the door and twined a muffler around her neck. Punkin', alerted by the familiar actions, was already on her feet and whining with excitement. Kristin couldn't stand to be cooped up inside for one more second.

"You're not going out in this weather?" Betsy queried from her spot in the rocker by the fireplace. "It's still snowing."

"I won't melt," Kristin snapped, and instantly regretted her peevishness. It was Gray she was mad at, Gray and herself and her stifled dreams, not a gentle soul like Betsy. "I'm sorry," Kristin muttered, feeling like she'd botched up one more thing in her life.

Outside Kristin forged into the swirling snow, reveling in the brisk, clean bite of the wind against her cheeks and ears. For the first time since Thanksgiving, she felt as if she could breathe again as she sucked cold drafts into her lungs. She tramped through the snow that had drifted into the ruts in the trail with no destination in mind. Punkin' cavorted at her heels, just as pleased as Kristin to be released from the claustrophobic confines of the room they shared. Kristin tucked her head down against the wind and watched her loden-green hiking boots stamp out prints in the snow as they carried her into the blessedly mind-numbing storm. Maybe it was the wind stinging her eyes that allowed the tears she'd forbidden to fall to begin flowing. Whatever the cause, Kristin was able to finally stop castigating herself for being a fool—for her stupidity in caring enough for Gray Lowrey to allow him to hurt her—and to let the tears she'd kept sealed up within her fall at last.

Kristin couldn't have said how long she'd been walking when she noticed that the snow was no longer falling around her in solid curtains of gray but had slowed to individual flakes that pirouetted slowly to earth. She glanced up. The day had lost the dense, closed-in feeling that comes with foul weather and was gradually opening up with a thin haze of light that filtered through the clearing clouds. Like the light from a high stained-glass cathedral window, the isolated rays burst through the pines in shafts of radiance.

Though Kristin had skied and hiked every trail in the lodge's vicinity during her first month at High Country, she initially didn't recognize where she was. As she looked around, she felt like a child creeping downstairs at dawn on Christmas morning. That same air of unearthly quiet and breath-holding anticipation hovered over the land, and the presents Kristin viewed were already unwrapped. She'd stumbled into a confectioner's dreamland. The tall pines were frosted with an impossibly thick coating of white icing. The snowflakes still twirling in the air were transformed into flying sugar crystals as they floated through the shafts of light streaking through the forest.

Little by little the dark, brooding clouds were chased away by a sun eager to lay claim again to the high mountains that were its rightful domain. The golden rays added yet another dimension of enchantment to the scene around Kristin. Her tears had had a cathartic, cleansing effect and the mountains, bathed now in sparkling gold, seemed almost to be rejoicing with her that the gloom had lifted. The sun's benevolence made Kristin feel like an invalid just coming to the end of a long convalescence.

Gray had delayed her recovery, she concluded, but only temporarily. She glanced around her and tiny segments of the loveliness with which she was surrounded caught her eye—a chubby, nose-high pine backlighted by an isolated beam of sunshine; a branch covered in hoarfrost so fantastic that crystalline patterns resembling icy feathers had formed on its needles; the way snow collected in the grooves of a ponderosa pine's bark, making the tree seem as if it were covered in lacy white scrollwork. Kristin soaked in the solitude and beauty of the scene for a long while. But it was only when she felt an undeniable urge rising in her that she knew she was finally on the way to becoming whole again. She wanted to photograph every precious detail.

"Come on, Punkin'." She hailed her truest companion, who was happily occupied rolling in the feathery snow like a bird taking a dust bath. "It's been too long between photo outings for us." Kristin hurriedly followed her waffled footprints back to the lodge, flew upstairs, loaded film into her camera, and was back outside before the snow on her parka had begun to melt.

The light, the condition of the snow, everything was perfect. Kristin connected instantly with that perfection the moment she put her eye to the camera's viewfinder and framed up a composition with the lacy hoarfrost. It seemed as if a missing link had been resoldered as Kristin lost herself in the world she perceived through the camera's eye. Kristin followed Punkin' farther into the forest.

They found a tree whose bark had been pierced by insects or birds or perhaps even frost. Kristin deduced that its berry-colored sap must have somehow leaked out for the bark was encrusted with strange purplish formations that reminded her of stalactites formed of grape Popsicles. She recorded the anomaly and moved on. Punkin' led her to a stream. Its edges were caked with ice, but a thin rivulet in the center was still running. The iced-over limbs of shaggy salt cedars hung above it like a ghostly apparition rattling in the wind. There was such an eerie quality to the scene that Kristin yearned for some way to interpret it, knowing that a straightforward rendering could never do it justice. Then an idea came to her. She dug through her film bag hoping that the roll she was looking for was still there. It was. She retrieved a canister of heat-sensitive, infrared film.

The only problem was that such a sensitive film had to be loaded into the camera in complete darkness. Kristin considered the difficulty for a moment, then shucked off her parka and improvised a hasty darkroom by wrapping the jacket around her camera and the film. With her hands out of sight, she fumbled with the film. Her cold-numbed fingers didn't make the job any easier, but finally she managed to engage the film on the take-up sprockets, clicked off a few frames, and snapped the camera shut. She hastily pulled her parka back on and attached the red filter necessary to photograph with infrared film. It was an unpredictable medium and Kristin shot the whole roll, not knowing whether she was actually capturing the unearthly beauty around her or merely conducting an interesting experiment.

The light was fading as Kristin started back. As if to welcome her home, nature had arranged a special treat that evening. "Alpenglow." Kristin breathed aloud the name of the rare phenomenon. She'd never witnessed it before, though she'd read about it many times. She remembered that the spectral display occurs only at the highest altitudes in snow-locked mountains when the sunset reflects off of the western slopes and makes the snow come alive with a reddish-lavender shimmer that lasts less than a minute. Shaking herself out of her bedazzled wonderment, Kristin whipped out her extra camera body in time to click off several shots of a snowscape glimmering with the haunting loveliness of the rare pastel hue. A few seconds later, the muted brilliance disappeared, reminding Kristin to hurry back to the lodge, because night was a cruel time in the mountains and it was approaching with a terrifying swiftness.

"My gosh, Kristin," Betsy exclaimed as Kristin reentered the lodge, "did you just win the lottery or find the pot of gold at the end of the rainbow? You look ecstatic about something."

Kristin laughed as she held up her frozen fingers to the fire. She felt the healthy, satisfied glow Betsy must have been referring to sparkling her cheeks. "I just stomped around long enough outside to clear the cobwebs out of my head. Listen," she went on, moving to Betsy's side, "I really am sorry I snapped at you earlier and that I've been such a grump for the past couple of weeks."

Betsy waved her hand airily. "Not to worry, we've all been bitten by a touch of cabin fever. You know what we need?" she asked.

Kristin shook her head, unable to guess.

"A cabin-fever party."

"Sounds like a positively inspired idea." Kristin

concurred wholeheartedly. Addie, Eric, the other staff members, and the handful of guests who'd been stranded at the lodge and were happily waiting until the snow-plows could reach them all eagerly joined in to give life to Betsy's inspiration. Soon steaming mugs of hot mulled wine were being passed around as everyone invaded the kitchen to prepare a dish that reflected his or her heritage. A businessman and his wife, both of Greek ancestry, contributed a tray of baklava rich with honey and butter. Kristin improvised on a spicy Scandinavian hors d'oeuvre that her father always prepared for special events. Eric and Betsy collaborated on Irish soda bread in honor of Betsy's Celtic background.

"If we had gone with my heritage," Eric quipped, "you would have been up all night waiting for my bagels, and I don't know where we would have gotten lox here on the top of a mountain in the middle of WASP land."

A couple of the local staff members created a savory, cumin-scented platter of enchiladas.

"I'm your basic Heinz Fifty-seven-variety-type person," Addie confessed. "I know I've got a lot of Cherokee circulating around my bloodstream, but I'm afraid I'd be hard-pressed to come up with buffalo steaks. Aside from that, I'm part German, French, Irish, Mexican, and a little bit of anything else you'd care to name."

"Sounds like a background as American as apple pie," Eric said, toasting her with his mug of wine.

"I guess that decides it then," Addie concluded, hauling out the apples and flour.

A crazy quilt of a feast followed, with nutrition and artful flavor combinations going by the wayside. The highlight of the evening came when Betsy and Eric recruited volunteers to join them in singing medieval madrigals.

"I don't know much about these here madrigals," Addie admitted warily, "but I put in many a year with the First Baptist choir back home." With the Greek businessman offering to carry the bass parts, the quartet embarked on some surprisingly good four-part harmonies.

"I guess music's music," Addie concluded, "whether you're singing about being washed in the blood of the Lamb or some *lydee faire*."

Simple as they were, the spur-of-the-moment festivities went a long way toward relieving the snowbound dreariness that had been dampening spirits; everyone headed for bed with snatches of madrigals humming through their brains.

The next morning Kristin awoke to the grind of the snowplows as the mechanical behemoths made their way up the mountains. She dressed quickly and collected all the rolls of film she'd shot the day before.

"Where are you headed off for so early?" Addie quizzed her as she bounced downstairs.

"I'm going to try to locate a darkroom in Taos," Kristin

answered, tugging on her gloves. "I doubt that any new guests will be arriving today, certainly not enough for a class, so I didn't think you'd mind."

"Lordy, child, you're not an indentured servant. You haven't been to town once since you started working up here. Not that I can see why anyone would want to spend any more time in so-called civilization than he absolutely has to. But no, of course I don't mind. I didn't know you were a photographer."

Kristin shrugged. "I don't know that I am," she answered, more truthfully than Addie could have ever known. "I just took some pictures and I want to see how they turned out; that's all."

"Well, be careful on those roads. They'll be iced up slicker than a skating rink and littered with fool Texans who don't know how to drive on anything not covered with dust or sand."

Kristin chuckled as she made her way down the mountain and saw the hulks of abandoned cars driven into banks of snow. Almost without exception the license plates were Texan. In Taos, Kristin started her inquiries at a photographic equipment store not too far from the plaza. After a few dead ends, she finally found an elderly photographer more than happy to rent out his rarely used darkroom. It was housed in what had once been a garage attached to his sprawling adobe hacienda on the west side of Taos. Kristin had worked in enough darkrooms that familiarizing herself with yet another new one didn't present any problems.

Half an hour later, she was lost in total darkness as her practiced hands fed film onto stainless-steel developing reels, then put the reels into light-tight tanks. Her nervousness mounted as she sloshed the developing chemicals around in the tanks, knowing that the negatives were taking form within. After she had fixed the images so they wouldn't fade in the light, Kristin was able to take the long strips of film out of the canister. She held the still-wet strip up to the light. Her long experience allowed her to "read" the negative, translating black to white and white to black. She couldn't tell for sure, but looking at the strip of infrared film, she was fairly certain that the efforts of the day before had been more than an interesting experiment.

She filled trays with more chemical solutions and unwrapped the package of photographic paper she'd purchased. She took the negatives from the drying cabinet and located the most promising one, a vertical portrayal of the icy stream. She switched on the enlarger, slid the negative in under the condenser, and focused the image that was magnified onto the eleven-by-fourteen-inch easel below. She turned off the enlarger light, slipped in a sheet of paper, and made the exposure.

In spite of how much work film photography was, Kristin wouldn't have traded the moment when, nearly trembling with anticipation, she slid the blank paper into the developing solution for all the digital images in the world. After several seconds a faint image appeared. Kristin was as excited as she'd been the first time she'd witnessed the chemical magic that brought a picture to ghostly life in front of her very eyes, then filled in the phantom tracing with solid blacks and grays. Though the amber-colored light that illuminated the darkroom was quite dim, Kristin could see enough to make her heart leap. It was there! She'd gotten it; she'd successfully caught the fairyland quality of the scene. Mesmerized by the bewitching power of the chemistry at work, she stared at the image she had created.

The infrared film had transformed the trickle of a stream into a viscous, black rivulet of ink. The icicle-laden branches had metamorphosed into a million rioting prisms radiating a blurred effervescence of light. In contrast to their dazzling luminescence, the stream looked as dark as if it were flowing chocolate syrup. It was simply not possible to achieve such richness digitally. As fast as she could, Kristin printed several other variations of the scene, and each one carried the same impact as the first.

The color film was a bit trickier to process and it was several hours before Kristin could finally view again the alpenglow. Its pastel delicacy was every bit as moving as the more vividly etched black-and-white prints, but in a subtler way that evoked a more complex string of emotions. Kristin followed that string and found that it led her to an immensely fulfilling terminus. It was the realization that this moment, as she hovered over a soupy chemical bath swirling a print around a dimly lighted tray in a drafty converted garage that still smelled of gasoline and oil, this moment was what counted. The moment when she knew she'd accomplished what she'd set out to do was the important one. Whether any other ever followed it, whether she ever won critical or popular acclaim, whether any other human even saw her work, was entirely secondary.

With a great satisfied sigh, Kristin packed up her prints and headed back up the mountain. The lodge was dark by the time she finally made her way up over the slick roads. Once inside, she realized that she hadn't eaten all the long day she'd spent cloistered in the dark. She headed for the kitchen, hoping to find some leftovers from dinner. In a warming tray by the stove was a plate that Addie had put aside for her. Digging in hungrily, Kristin was halfway through with the meal before she noticed the note Addie had tucked under her fork. She unfolded it and read:

If you're reading this, I suppose it means you made your way home safely. Hope you like what I saved for you. I figured you'd be hungry.

Don't know if you want to know or even care, but thought I should warn you anyhow. Gray and Laurie will be here next week to spend the Christmas holidays.

Hasta mañana,
Addie

Chapter 7

In the weeks preceding Christmas, Kristin stole every moment she could to wander alone exploring back trails and gaining new perspectives on familiar scenes. More than ever before, she sought out the solace she'd always found in the mountain's snowy isolation. And always she brought along two companions, Punkin' and her camera. Just as strongly as she had felt an aversion to photography after her show, she now experienced a near compulsion to record the land around her and its impact upon her. As often as she could, she made the treacherous journey down the mountain to her rented darkroom to learn what her solitary forays had yielded.

One snowy evening, she was leaving the darkroom and happened to glance into the adobe house to which it was linked. She saw the man she'd rented the darkroom from and a couple with a child, a grandchild, clustered around a gaily decorated tree. The lights and tinsel on the tree lent it a radiance that made Kristin think of the luminosity of her infrared photos. The child was obviously freshly bathed and was wearing one-piece pajamas with feet attached. All three adults beamed as the child toddled to the tree and began unwrapping a present.

It's Christmas Eve, Kristin thought, stunned that she could have lost track of time so completely. With a start she realized that her memory lapse was probably not entirely accidental. Her subconscious had been keeping the date at bay to protect her from the inevitable turmoil it signaled, because Christmas meant Gray's arrival.

As she feared, his Bronco sat outside the lodge when Kristin returned. She left the prints she'd just completed in the back of her Volvo. She wanted to be free to move as swiftly as she possibly could through the main hall, hopefully unnoticed.

"There you are, Kristin," Addie announced as she stepped inside the door. "We were afraid you'd miss the festivities. Come on in. Grab some eggnog. We're about to start opening the presents."

Presents? Kristin wondered. She was the only one who regularly left the lodge; how could there be presents? But her puzzling was stopped dramatically as a cherubic figure in powder-blue corduroy ran up to grab her legs.

"Laurie, hello." Kristin kneeled down to greet the little girl and return her hug. She was startled by the surge of affection that shot through her as she cradled the small, sturdy body against her own.

"Punkin'!" Laurie exclaimed as the big dog came up to sniff at her. She dissolved in peals of delighted laughter when a friendly canine tongue found her cheek. "A doggie kiss, Daddy! Did you see the doggie kiss me?"

Kristin watched the shadowed spot Laurie ran to and saw the hard angles of Gray's face emerge. Illuminated again in firelight, they brought a powerful reminder to Kristin of the last time she'd seen that face, above hers, lighted by the flickers from the embers in the office fireplace.

"Hello, Kristin." His greeting was low and gentle, as if he spoke to her from across the length of a pillow as they awoke together on a spring morning.

Everyone else in the room vanished as Kristin's eyes found Gray's. She didn't trust herself to speak and merely nodded in reply. She read a silent plea in the velvety depths of his eyes, but she couldn't interpret it, not completely. Its surface message was obvious, however; he wanted her to come to him. That she wouldn't do. No matter how strongly she was drawn to him—and the undeniable power of their mutual attraction made itself felt with a fierce intensity in that moment—she couldn't jeopardize the small reserves of emotional strength she'd managed to build up over the past few weeks. They were too precious—no, essential—to her psychic survival.

Hands tugged at her parka. "Here, let me take that before you start dripping like a wet hound," Addie joked, relieving the slight tension that had been building as Kristin stood speechless before the gathering. "And you take this," the lodge manager added, slipping a cup of eggnog into Kristin's hand. Kristin shakily found her way to an empty chair as "Santa Claus"—Eric in a pair of red flannel long johns and a beard of white yarn—began dispensing the presents that had materialized as mysteriously as the Christmas tree they surrounded.

"First delivery is for Miss Laurie Lowrey," Eric announced, presenting a package wrapped in red foil to Laurie. Her almond-slanted eyes lighted up. "From Betsy." Eric read the card for the little girl as Laurie painstakingly pulled the wrapping away. Inside was a doll that Betsy had fashioned from yarn.

"A doll!" Laurie whooped. "I'm going to call her Betsy." At that moment it would have been difficult to say who was more pleased with the gift, Laurie or a softly smiling Betsy. More of Betsy's yarn creations followed: a sweater featuring reindeer leaping across the chest for Eric, mittens for Addie, a muffler for Gray, and a saucy tam in kelly green for Kristin.

"I thought the color would be nice with your hair," Betsy explained.

"It's gorgeous," Kristin said, modeling the cap.

Next up was Eric's handiwork. Even Betsy was surprised to discover that he'd abandoned his chess set and spent the last few weeks fashioning a different set of gnomes. Everyone received one of the lovably ugly creatures carved with his or her own likeness, or a rough caricature anyway. Addie's presents came, naturally, from the kitchen as boxes of fudge, peanut brittle, and divinity for her High Country Lodge family. Gray's gifts were the only store-bought ones—new skis for Eric, a calculator to help Addie with her bookwork, recordings of medieval madrigals for Betsy, and a bright red sled and some other carefully chosen toys for Laurie. For Punkin' he'd brought a selection of the most succulent steak bones from his Powderhorn restaurant, Le Piste Rouge.

Kristin joined in the laughter as the golden retriever attacked the meaty bones, but her joviality was forced. Two thoughts tore at her: She had no presents to give anyone and Gray had conspicuously absented her name from his gift list. A sudden inspiration solved the first problem.

Kristin raced first outside to the car to gather up her new prints, then upstairs. She hadn't intended to show her photographs to anyone, but this occasion warranted a special response. Almost as if she'd planned it, she found prints that could have been taken especially for each of the people so dear to her. The picture of the lacy scrollwork on the side of the ponderosa pine seemed to fit Betsy and her love of intricate musical and knitting patterns. There was a picture of a lonely, remote trail that Eric had told her was one of his favorites. Kristin was sure he'd like having a photographic remembrance of it. The photo of the feathery hoarfrost somehow reminded Kristin of Addie's kindness and how it had flourished in High Country's harsh elements. Punkin' frolicking in the powdery snow seemed the perfect choice for Laurie. There was one other print that Kristin felt was a perfect match for someone downstairs—the alpenglow print. But she put it aside. She couldn't give it to Gray. Not in front of everyone. Not after he'd chosen to leave her off his gift list. She bundled up the chosen photographs and rushed downstairs.

The silence after Kristin had distributed her prints grew so uncomfortably long that she was forced to conclude she'd made a terrible mistake. "I'm sorry. I didn't have time to wrap them," she faltered.

"I'm not." Gray's voice issued from the dark corner. "Wrapping would have made it that much harder for me to see them, and these photographs are something I wouldn't have wanted to miss. Kristin, they are really remarkable."

Gray's judgment snapped them all out of the trances they seemed to have fallen into while gazing at their prints. "He's right," Addie agreed, her voice an awed whisper. "Lordy, I knew you'd been taking pictures, but I had no idea that you were a for-real artist."

The others joined in expressing their astonished gratitude. But it was Gray's reaction that had touched Kristin most deeply, perhaps because her work appeared to have affected him so intensely. He went from one print to the next, studying each one in microscopic detail. As the group disbanded, heading toward the kitchen to mix up another batch of eggnog, Gray approached Kristin.

Speaking low, he faced her. "I meant what I said. Your work is something quite special. Taos is a town full of photographers, but what I've seen tonight is far beyond what they're doing." Gray's earnest words tumbled out almost against his will.

"I looked at those photos and . . ." Gray paused, his hands reaching in front of him as if for a concept he couldn't put into words. "And I saw the mountains, the way I see them, the way I love them."

Kristin was at a loss as she fumbled to react to the onslaught of Gray's response. It was the response she had always yearned for but had failed to elicit from Dennis Hascomb or any other man she had ever been close to. She couldn't help noting the irony of her situation—now that she had the response, she didn't have the man. Still, Gray's praise meant more to her than she cared to admit. Far more than was healthy for her.

"How long have you been photographing?" he asked.

"For several years now," Kristin admitted.

"Why aren't you pursuing it professionally? You're certainly good enough."

Kristin glanced backward to the kitchen, where the others had congregated. She wasn't sure she was ready yet to talk about her first show, but she certainly wasn't ready to have it become general knowledge. "Actually," she began hesitantly, "I was doing just that. I had my first one-woman exhibit a few weeks before I came up here."

"And?" Gray prompted her, leaning disturbingly close to hear her murmured words.

"And it was a flop," Kristin stated flatly. "The art reviewer for the local paper said my photos left a cloying aftertaste. I guess the art-buying public agreed with her because no one bought anything from the show. The gallery closed it a couple of weeks early."

"And you turned tail and ran for the mountains."

Kristin was startled by the vehemence of Gray's statement. It was a shock after the apparent closeness of the bond her work had forged between them. "I would hardly call it turning tail," she hissed, trying to keep her voice from reaching the crowd in the kitchen. "I would call it more a strategic withdrawal. I didn't feel like picking up a camera again for a good long while."

"Why?" Gray continued his brutal interrogation. "Just because one sour critic didn't like your work? Seems pretty weakhearted to me to give up on your art because one person turned thumbs down on it."

Goaded beyond endurance, Kristin retaliated. "I don't see that it's any more weakhearted than what you've done," she snapped, the gray flecks in her eyes heating to sizzling sparks of rage. "You've turned tail and run from half the human race just because one sour critic, your wife, gave *you* the thumbs down. I mean, we're both hiding out, aren't we, Gray? The only difference is that it's temporary for me, but it appears that you're a permanent emotional exile."

Gray sagged visibly as Kristin's words bit into him. Kristin felt as if she'd physically struck him but knew any blow she could have delivered wouldn't have hit him as hard as her words had. Although she'd felt they had been justified, she now bitterly regretted her harsh words. It was too late to take them back, however, and besides, she reminded herself sternly, Gray Lowrey had wounded *her* more than once.

"I deserved that," Gray said, his voice now carrying only a hollow echo of the animation it had contained moments before. "I shouldn't have spoken the way I did. It's just that I couldn't help myself when I thought about all the no-talents, frauds, and one-dimensional fakes out there cluttering up gallery walls and getting famous with their vacuous work, and here you are perched up on top of a mountain with the best photography of this area I've ever seen hidden away in your room."

"Thanks," Kristin said, relieved that her barbed words didn't seem to have had any lasting effect. "I'm sorry about what I said too."

"No," Gray contradicted her, "after what's happened between you and me, I can see how you might have reached the conclusions you have and, in a way, you're right. In another way you're completely wrong, but that's beside the point."

Kristin wanted to blurt out that what had happened between him and his ex-wife was precisely the point, because it seemed to have completely mucked up whatever relationship might have existed between *them*. But she held her tongue. There had been enough outbursts for one evening, and the reasons why nothing could develop between them had long since been relegated to past history. All Kristin hoped for now was that they could have a cordial, if somewhat cool, friendship that wouldn't mar the rest of her time at High Country.

"More to the point is that you've got talent, Kristin, real talent." Gray said the words with utter authority, as if his opinion were as undeniable as gravity. His unshakable confidence filled Kristin with a warmth that heated all the cold, musty spots where the insecurities and doubts planted by her first show had taken root. "And it shouldn't be rotting away up here. Listen"—he leaned forward again, reenergized—"I've got a friend who's setting up a show to open on New Year's Eve. He owns a highly respected gallery and wouldn't consider exhibiting you unless he absolutely believed in your stuff. I mean, I could arrange a meeting for tomorrow morning, but he wouldn't take you on as a favor to me or to the queen of England or to anyone else. Do you have any other prints besides the ones I saw tonight?"

Kristin nodded, thinking of the ones she'd left upstairs. "I also have extra prints of the four I gave away."

"Great," Gray exclaimed enthusiastically. "Mind if I have a look at them later, after I've gotten Laurie to bed? I'd hate to find out that you're a four-photo fluke."

"That *would* be embarrassing," Kristin replied mockingly. Determined to inaugurate their cordial, yet cool, friendship, she added in a deliberately breezy tone, "Sure, most of them are up in my room. Stop by later on and you can decide whether or not you think I rate an introduction to your friend."

"You rate, Kristin; there's no doubt about that."

She turned from him quickly, before she could allow herself to read a double meaning into his words. She knew she couldn't survive the winter if she insisted on nourishing herself with scraps of false hope.

Upstairs, she unpacked all the prints she'd kept tucked away under her bed and arranged them across the blue gingham of the comforter. When all the space on the bed was taken, she propped the photos up on every available piece of furniture. Kristin didn't realize just how much work she'd completed until she was literally surrounded by the pieces. As she waited for Gray, she steadfastly refused to change out of the clothes she wore, although they carried a whiff of darkroom chemicals and the front of her sweater was dotted with brown spots from where she'd dribbled fixer on it. She forbade herself to even run a brush through her hair. She wanted to dramatically illustrate, to herself as much as to Gray, that she fully intended their relationship to be a platonic one.

So, an impish thought pricked her, *why are you jumping at the sound of a firm rap on your door?* Kristin pushed aside the pointed observation and went to answer the knock.

"Hey," Gray said exuberantly, surveying the display, "you've created quite the little gallery in here. Oh, these are good," he muttered, transfixed by the photos. "Really good." He picked up each print, lingering over the hazy pastels and luminous black and whites, cradling them in his arms as he went. At the end of his tour, he had every one scooped into his arms. Carrying them with a touching delicacy, he settled into an armchair and began to pore over the collection again.

"It's all here," he announced. "Everything I've ever felt about the high country and could never possibly have expressed. It's all here," he muttered again, unable to drag his attention away from the prints. "I can't wait to show this stuff to Harrell." He glanced up at Kristin, who had found a perch on the edge of the bed. "That's Harrell Langston. He owns the gallery I mentioned earlier."

"Not the Langston Gallery," Kristin gasped.

"Yes, why? Is there something wrong with it?"

"Wrong? I read about that gallery in my art books at college. Harrell Langston is part of art history."

"Harrell won't be terribly flattered to find out that he's already history." The laugh they shared ended in an unguarded moment in which they both found themselves looking a bit too long and too hard at each other. To break what was becoming a threateningly intimate moment, Gray looked away. His exuberance faded as his gaze went from the blue gingham curtains to the comforter. With all the photos down, he seemed to be seeing the room for the first time. His tone was somber when he spoke again. "I haven't been in this room for—" He abruptly halted his calculations with a curt, "A long time."

"Not since your wife left, right?" The impulsive honesty that guided so much of what she did and was caused Kristin to blurt out the words. She was tired of hedging warily around the subject.

"Exactly." Gray sighed, almost as if it were a relief for him to make the admission. In a wistful tone, he continued. "She never liked this room. Hated the way Addie and I fixed it up for her. Said all the blue gingham was too hickish for her." A dry snort of laughter punctuated the comment. "I had planned that we'd live up here after Laurie was born. High Country always seemed to me to be the ideal place to raise a child. So much better than Powderhorn with its jet-set retinue. But Jan had other ideas."

Gray looked down at the prints that, moments before, had been strewn across the bed that he had once shared with his wife. But Kristin knew he wasn't seeing them; his inner eye was focused on memories nearly a decade old. Like a man who for years refuses to talk about his wartime experiences, then can't stop once he finally begins, Gray went on.

"She spent about two nights here, then made her hickish statement, packed up, and left for Powderhorn. She was partying and skiing almost up to the day Laurie was born. Christ, she was a beautiful woman." The statement came out with a forlorn despair.

Kristin had no luck in forbidding the cruel slice of jealousy's claws as she listened to Gray reminisce.

"And didn't she know it too," he added darkly. "Knew it and expected beauty to make her fortune for her. Maybe she was always the person I finally saw in the end, maybe it was that expectation that curdled her, soured whatever I thought I'd once loved in her."

Once loved. The words ricocheted through Kristin's

brain. "What do you mean, Gray?" she asked gently, feeling that if she spoke too loudly she might wake Gray from the almost trancelike state he appeared to be in.

"I mean, after Laurie was born, and even before, she changed. Either changed or allowed her real self to show through the veneer of beauty covering her. During the pregnancy *I* was the one who went around glowing like the proverbial expectant mother. Jan took it as a nine-month sentence literally culminating in hard labor."

Again Gray laughed dryly, but his artificial amusement couldn't hide from Kristin the anguish and disappointment behind his words.

"During those months, we seemed to drift farther and farther apart until she was a stranger to me. A stranger who was carrying my child. Jan hated the baby before she was even born for ruining her figure, for restricting her freedom. At nights I'd lie next to Jan and try to stroke her belly to let our child know that she was loved."

Kristin felt her breath clogging her chest as she imagined Gray expressing his love to his unborn child.

"When it came time for the delivery, Jan demanded that she be knocked out. When she came to, she didn't even ask if she'd had a boy or a girl. Didn't even ask." Gray reiterated the words, his hurt bewilderment still fresh after eight years. "When they brought Laurie to her, Jan wasn't interested in breast-feeding her. From the start she rejected her own child, our child. Then, when

I told her that our baby had Down syndrome, Jan refused to even hold her. I thought that she might be going through some kind of postpartum depression, so I tried to understand and support Jan and also to be as much of a mother as I could to Laurie." Gray glanced up to gauge Kristin's reaction to his tale.

"I'm not saying that I wasn't disappointed. I was confused myself at first. You know, for nine months I'd fantasized about the perfect child we were going to have and the perfect family we were going to be. But when I saw Laurie, held her, any disappointment vanished. She was Laurie and I loved her the way she was.

"I was certain that Jan eventually would too. She never did. If it hadn't been for Addie, Laurie could have starved to death for all Jan cared." The memory was etched in vitriol and Gray didn't try to hide his bitterness. Kristin saw quite clearly that, far from revering his ex-wife, Gray despised her.

"Jan was the perfect beauty who couldn't deal with having borne a less-than-perfect child. Though emotionally Jan had abandoned Laurie before she was even born, she hung around for four years, long enough for Laurie to become attached in spite of her chilling indifference. I'm not sure why Jan stayed that long—probably waiting for the best offer. It finally came in the form of this flashy Los Angeles producer who Jan invited to one of the countless little soirees she was always hosting for what she considered the 'right' people. Anyway, he promised her movie stardom and guaranteed that he could make her fondest dream in life come true. You know what that dream was?" Gray inquired caustically.

Kristin shook her head in a silent negative.

"To see her face on the cover of *People* magazine." He shook his head wearily, as if trying to rattle the inane image loose. "Well, old Jan never made it to the cover, but she can sure be seen often enough in the back pages. That producer didn't get Jan the film contracts he'd promised, so she dumped him and has relied on her face and figure to make her a star of television commercials, pushing everything from foot powder to shampoo. That lovely, lovely face finally did make Jan her fortune." Gray's tone left no doubt as to what he thought of the person behind the face.

"Laurie," Gray went on, his voice softening at his daughter's name, "was crushed. She couldn't understand why her mother would leave without even saying good-bye. In spite of the way Jan had neglected her, Laurie was deeply attached to her. Maybe she was just attached to the idea of having a mother. Whatever it was, I can't count the number of times she woke up crying for her mommy. I think she's over the worst of the rejection now, but," Gray concluded with a sudden vehemence, "by God, I'll never let anyone hurt her that way again."

At last, Kristin understood the emotional barriers

Gray had constructed to protect himself and his daughter. For several long moments neither of them spoke. All the disturbing emotions that Kristin had attempted to keep trapped within herself burst free, churning up in a roiling mass of confusion. One fact broke away to float on the surface like the bit of wreckage that a drowning man clings to. Kristin didn't stop to consider whether she made any sense or was totally off the mark.

"I'm not Jan," she whispered.

Those three simple words cut through to the heart of Gray's story as it affected both their lives in the present. "No, you're not," he agreed with an equal simplicity.

"But can't you see what you're doing?" Kristin protested. "You're making me pay for what she did."

A furrowed intensity shielded Gray's features and Kristin couldn't tell if he understood what she was saying. Suddenly, it became urgently important for her to get her message across.

"For some reason I can't fathom," she continued breathlessly, "you've equated the two of us. Maybe you've equated every woman you've met since she left with Jan. That's what I meant when I said you were an emotional exile. I can see now why it happened. You were hurt, Gray. She betrayed you, your child, and your dreams. But that's her. We're not all vain, flighty, and faithless, you know."

"I know, Kristin; believe me, I know. And I'm not so

unacquainted with the slightly battered workings of my own mind to be unaware of what you're saying. When you threw my words back in my face, the ones about letting one sour critic ruin my life, they were right on target and hit a very sensitive bull's-eye."

Kristin stared at him. She hadn't known what sort of response her irrepressible honesty would elicit, but she hadn't been prepared for Gray's total agreement with her analysis. He studied his hands, seeming almost surprised to find them empty. With a decisive abruptness he knitted them together.

"Do you think," he asked, wrenching the words from himself, "that I haven't wondered myself why I haven't been able to sustain a relationship with a woman since Jan left? I know that a lot of people—I think Addie is one of them; you might have been—think that I'm still mourning for Jan, still clinging to her memory somehow." Gray's mouth, a full-lipped slash beneath his dark mustache, curled with contempt for the idea. "Nothing could be farther from the truth."

"Then what is it?" Kristin asked, struggling to keep her voice even to maintain the slender pretense that her interest was academic, that it didn't really involve her at all. She waited for his answer the way a man on trial waits for the judge's sentence.

"It took me a while to figure out myself. I finally had to stand back and dispassionately examine this cycle I was repeating over and over with the women who were, however briefly, a part of my life. Finally it became clear."

Kristin's breath grew shallow as she waited for the verdict.

"I was attracted to women, naturally enough, by their beauty. It's something that I don't seem able to change even if I want to, but that's the precise quality that makes it impossible for me to trust them."

"But that's—"

Gray held up a hand to deflect the protest he was interrupting. "Illogical?" he quizzed. "Of course it is. But those are the hard ones, aren't they?" he asked grimly, already knowing the answer. "Sane, orderly problems are easy. They can be attacked and solved just the way I'd solve any problem I run into here or at Powderhorn. No, it's the illogical ones that are hard, that can't be rooted out because they exist in some musty corner of the mind that reason can't touch." Sinewy cords stood out at the back of Gray's hands as he made a fist and ground it into the palm of his other hand.

"Look"—his eyes swung to grab hers—"this is ridiculous, talking as if this is some abstract problem removed from us. It's you and I that I'm talking about. Us. Why it won't work. Why I wish like hell it could, but it won't. I know. I've seen what's happened too many times with too many women. You're too special, Kristin. I could never allow that to happen to you."

An odd kind of relief flooded over Kristin. His tortured words had released her from all her theorizing and from the painful conclusion that he simply hadn't cared. It was clear that his ruthless honesty had come at a great cost, and Kristin felt honored that he'd considered her worth the price. Still, she had to be sure, to know decisively that there was no chance. With an uncharacteristic timidity, she asked, "But, if I'm so special, why couldn't it be different?"

"I thought it could," Gray answered, continuing to match her spontaneous honesty with his own. "But your beauty keeps getting in the way. As much as it attracts me, when I stop and really look at you, something inside of me withers with terror."

Kristin couldn't suppress a burst of dry, ironic laughter. "This is funny," she said, facetiously choosing the last adjective that could aptly describe the situation. "All the time I was growing up, I dreamed of being beautiful. But there I was, this overgrown stalk of a girl, always a head taller than everyone, including the boys, in my classes. Then, later on, art, photography, became the only things that mattered to me and I sort of forgot about how I looked. Or, if I did think about beauty, being beautiful and all, it just seemed to me to be this kind of flimsy basket that any woman would be very stupid to put all her eggs in. Do you know what I mean?" she asked Gray, grappling to put a concept into words for the first time.

"I mean beauty, looks, they don't last, so I considered them silly things to be much concerned about. Women who *do* worry about them just seem to be guaranteeing themselves a lot of misery when the inevitable wrinkles arrive."

"Kristin, no matter whether you think you are or not, or whether you even much care, you're a very beautiful woman. You can't change that any more than I can seem to change this illogical, neurotic response I have to it." He leaned forward in the chair as if reaching out for her understanding. "This hasn't been easy for me. I just wanted you to understand why things are the way they have to be. I don't want to hurt you." There was a strangled kind of suffering so evident in his last sentence that Kristin ached to go to him, to wrap her arms around the broad, strapping shoulders that were now slumped and defeated looking.

"I do understand, Gray," she said, hating the words that would take him away from her forever, but feeling she had no other choice. With or without her understanding, Gray Lowrey was never going to be a part of her life. "And it means a great deal to me that you explained everything to me." Deep within her, the desire that Gray had sparked smoldered. It warmed her as she looked at him and remembered the feel of his lips on hers, the delicious tickle of his beard. A flame licked at the edges of the coolly detached facade behind which she was hiding her feelings. She yearned to give herself up to the seductive heat but knew that it would utterly consume her and destroy the fragile friendship that Gray was attempting to construct between them.

There was a hard set to Gray's full mouth as he returned her gaze, as if he too were struggling to restrain lips that longed to taste again the fiery sweetness that they had savored together. Kristin knew that a move, a gesture, from her and the desire that flickered between them would ignite, so powerful was the force of their mutual attraction. It hummed through the room, filling the air with a highly charged tension. Kristin yearned for the release that she knew she would find only locked in Gray's arms, the thunder of his heartbeat resonating through every cell in her body.

If you go to him now, came a warning issued from a cooler island of reason in some remote part of her mind, *you will deserve whatever heartache you get. If you deliberately crumble the walls of his resolve after he has struggled to build them to protect you, you will have earned the suffering you endure when those walls tumble down on you.* Hoping to absorb strength from the molecules of oxygen floating in the air, Kristin inhaled a steadying lungful.

"Have you seen as much of my work as you need to?" she asked shakily.

Gray's gaze dropped to the prints lying forgotten on

his lap. Awkwardly, he thumbed through them again, seeming to collect his composure as he eyed the icy scenes. When he spoke again, his voice had its usual, almost brash, confidence.

"I love them all." He reconfirmed his earlier opinion. "But this one"—the timbre of his voice trailed off as he held the print up and mused almost to himself—"this one . . ."

It was the alpenglow photograph, the one Kristin herself had picked out for Gray but hadn't dared to present to him. "Funny you should especially like that one." Kristin attempted to pump a jovial lightness into her tone that she didn't feel. "I'd thought of giving it to you as a present."

"You did? Any particular reason?"

Kristin sensed that Gray already knew why she'd selected that one for him. For a second, a debate raged within her. In the end she decided to answer his question as honestly as he had hers.

"Because it captures a moment that was terribly brief. But a moment that graced my life with a loveliness I'd never known before. I treasure it for that. And now it's even more precious to me because I never expect to experience it again." Kristin knew that tears glistened, unshed, in her eyes, but she wasn't ashamed of Gray seeing them. She felt as if they'd come through a spiritual ordeal together and were close in a way that she'd never been close to anyone else before. Hers were tears of farewell, signaling her acceptance of what could never be between them.

Kristin saw a liquid shimmer in Gray's eyes as well before his glance skittered away. It was several moments before he spoke, his voice ragged. "Thank you. I'll treasure it for that same reason. And I," he said, putting the stack of prints carefully on the floor and twisting to the side to reach into his pants pocket, "have something for you too." He held up a chain of gleaming silver. A chunk of turquoise dangled from it. "It's from the old Cerrillos mine. It's been mined out for years, but I found this nugget and had it reset. For you. Because it reminded me of your eyes." He stumbled through the explanation. "Anyway, I didn't want to give it to you unless you wanted to hear and could understand what I had to say to you and could accept the necklace as a gift of friendship." He held it out to her. As he did so, his shirt sleeve rode up away from his sturdy wrist, revealing the bracelet that Kristin had admired the day they'd met. One of the three chunks of turquoise had been removed, leaving an empty socket of silver gaping open.

Forcing her hand to do what her heart forbade, Kristin reached out for the spiraling gem. For a moment the charcoal-veined piece of turquoise twirled and danced just beyond her grasp, then Gray lowered it slowly into her palm. The silver chain puddled in her outstretched hand like the shining boundaries of a dream that has collapsed inward on itself. Gray had already left, taking the alpenglow print and quietly closing the door behind him, by the time Kristin closed her fingers over the necklace.

Chapter 8

Sleep was a long time in coming that night. Kristin was reminded of the other restless Christmas Eves she'd spent as a young girl, straining to hear the clatter of eight tiny reindeer upon her rooftop. But there would be no happy surprises to wake up to this year. Only the prospect of meeting Harrell Langston the next day could keep thoughts of Gray at bay for sporadic bursts of time. Then prickles of nervous anticipation would replace the grief that deadened her spirit every time she veered too close to thoughts of what might have been.

She tried not to let any excitement build within her about the next day's possibilities: The work of very few was deemed good enough to grace the walls of the Langston Gallery. Then again, Kristin reminded herself, very few even got to *meet* the owner of that esteemed gallery. Contenting herself with the consolation of an introduction, Kristin slid into a shallow trough of sleep.

"Kristin, are you about ready?"

Gray's voice melded seamlessly into the dream she was having in which he was the lead character. It took several moments for her to rouse herself enough to realize that the pounding on her door was being done by the flesh-and-blood version.

"Just give me a few more minutes," she croaked in a sleep-roughened voice. In the emotional upheaval of the previous night, she'd forgotten to set her alarm.

"We need to be on the road in ten minutes or we'll be late," Gray cautioned patiently. "Do you still feel up to going?" His voice had the walking-on-eggs hesitancy people adopted when they addressed the sick or emotionally disturbed.

"Of course I feel up to going, you ninny," Kristin shot back with a forced comic feistiness. "It's not every day I get to meet a living legend."

"All right, then, shake your buns. The bus leaves in ten minutes."

Kristin breathed a sigh of relief. She couldn't have endured it if Gray had begun treating her like a psychological invalid, weighing every word he spoke to her. She had accepted the necklace she now wore around her neck in the spirit of friendship and she was going to act like a friend, not some moony scorned lover.

"Do you always drive this fast?" Kristin asked later,

clinging to the door handle of the high-riding Bronco as they screeched around a curve in the mountain road.

"Sorry," Gray apologized, gearing down to cut the vehicle's speed. "I'm so used to driving these roads alone that I forget that not everyone knows every twist and turn that's coming the way I do. Are you nervous?"

"About your driving or about meeting Harrell Langston?" she joked.

"How about 'all of the above'?"

"That would cover it," Kristin concurred. Hesitantly, she asked, "Is what I'm wearing all right?"

He slid a sideways glance toward her. His attention on her was as palpable as his touch had been. She regretted that she had invited his scrutiny as it took in her old standby jeans-and-cashmere-sweater ensemble.

"You look fine to me."

"That's fortunate, considering I have nothing else to wear other than ski clothes."

"Harrell would barely notice if you showed up in your nightgown. Taos is full of rich eastern expatriates and trust-fund cowboys who have nothing better to do with their money than spend it on clothes they think will convince everyone that they're really eccentric artists. Anyone who lives here very long just stops noticing altogether what people are wearing."

A flutter of nervousness rippled through Kristin's

stomach as they approached the outskirts of Taos. Along the way into the town, they passed open fields stacked with pyramids of hay and honeycombed with the tunneled burrows of countless prairie dogs. The sandy-haired creatures stood up on hind legs, their plump bellies exposed to a ruffling wind, to inspect the Bronco as it drove past. At the turnoff for the eight-hundred-year-old Taos Indian pueblo, Kristin wondered how the ancient four- and five-story adobe structures set against sacred Pueblo Mountain would look in an infrared rendering. The street leading into the main plaza was lined with tall cottonwoods. The closer they came to the heart of the city, the more the spaces between the cottonwoods came to be filled with boutiques featuring costly handcrafted clothing, overpriced restaurants, tourists frequenting both, and, above all, art galleries.

Kristin was overwhelmed by the number of galleries. *And Langston's is the best*, she thought, suddenly struck by the implications of that realization: She was aiming too high. A streak of panic shimmied through her. She should be starting out at one of the innumerable lesser galleries for her first show in an internationally known art center like Taos. What was she going to say to Mr. Langston when he asked about her previous exhibits? Tell him that she'd had one show that went over so badly it closed two weeks early? No, she couldn't mention her failure.

She looked over at Gray, his profile almost stonily impassive. Kristin thought of the intriguing bundle of contradictions hidden by that chiseled invulnerability. She wondered how many others had seen as many sides of Gray as she had, or even if there was any *one* other. She doubted there were many. The knowledge that she'd likely shared more with Gray than most had comforted her and now gave her the courage to suggest, "Maybe we shouldn't be doing this." The suggestion came out as a reedy whisper.

Gray looked over at her, alerted by the note of thinly disguised panic he'd discerned. One glance at Kristin confirmed his suspicion.

"I can understand your being nervous. But you're really good, I promise. Don't back out." His hand left the steering wheel and found Kristin's.

Kristin felt his hand settle on her own like a mother hen onto an egg. She was warmed and strengthened by his touch, his concern. Her doubts took wing like black crows scared away from a field of new corn. The feel of his hand on hers acted on Kristin like a transfusion of confidence.

"I won't," she said with a smile.

Gray withdrew his hand, not wanting to maintain the contact for a beat longer than simple friendship demanded. They parked and Kristin gathered up her prints, then followed Gray through a maze of adobe buildings to a courtyard set far back from the much-traveled tourist routes. The enclosing adobe wall had a white piping of snow rimming it. Kristin imagined that the peaceful courtyard must be lovely in the spring when the willows and the abundance of potted flowers were in bloom. Now, the walkway was lined with luminarias, paper bags filled with sand in which candles had flickered on Christmas Eve. These lit, according to legend, the way for the Baby Jesus to the gallery door, which was hung with a wreath of red chilies. The gallery itself was a simple, cloistered structure that made no special bids for attention. It was obvious that patrons came to the Langston Gallery; the Langston Gallery did not seek out patrons.

"Merry Christmas," a jolly figure called out as they entered. The man who'd greeted them looked like a counterculture Santa Claus with his long white hair, thinning on top, pulled back into a ponytail. He wore a faded blue work shirt pulled over a substantial paunch and tucked into baggy jeans. Topping the outfit was a king's ransom in antique turquoise and silver. The gallery was surprisingly large inside, with high ceilings supported by a herringbone pattern of exposed viga beams.

"Merry Christmas, Harrell," Gray replied, gripping the man's hand in a hearty shake.

So this is Harrell Langston, Kristin realized, delighted to find that she wasn't going to have to face some self-important snob in a three-piece suit.

"And you must be Kristin Jonsson," he said, warmly taking Kristin's hand. "I'm Harrell Langston. Welcome to my gallery."

The contrast Langston, an acknowledged great in the art world, made to Alana Moorington, was striking. Langston was as low-keyed, human, and unpretentious as Alana was postured and chilly.

"You're teaching up at High Country, right? How do you like it up there in the chilly heights?" he asked with the genuine interest of a favorite uncle.

"I love it," Kristin answered, all trace of nervousness and self-consciousness gone. "The chilly heights have always been some of my favorite places."

"And how are things at Powderhorn and your places down south?" Langston turned his kindly inquiry to Gray.

"Couldn't be better. We've gotten the snow we needed this year. Sort of makes up for last year's disaster. When are you coming up?"

"Just as soon as I get this next show sorted out, I'll be there trying to break some of my foolish old bones." He turned back to Kristin. "Gray tells me you have some prints I can't live another day without seeing."

Kristin unwrapped her bundle of photographs. Langston took them, laying them down on a large worktable. Kristin wondered about the work that had been spread across that table in the past forty years, during which time Langston had shown every major artist in the Southwest and beyond. She watched the ponytailed figure bend over her photographs, inspecting each print in absolute silence. Gone was the friendly uncle, replaced by the forceful man who had made the Langston Gallery what it was. Langston focused himself totally on the task of evaluating the work before him. He trained every sense on Kristin's prints, seeming even to use his sense of smell like a wine connoisseur, gauging the bouquet of the photographic emulsion.

The appraisal went on far too long. Kristin guessed why he was taking such an excessive amount of time poring over her prints—he was trying to frame a polite rejection, one that wouldn't offend his good and powerful friend Grayson Lowrey. She imagined that Langston would look up regretfully and say that, while her work showed extraordinary promise, she wasn't quite ready yet, but to be sure and come back to him in a few years and that he certainly appreciated them dropping by. Kristin was on the verge of saying something to ease the inevitable, to thank Harrell Langston for his time and reveal that she never really expected that anything would come of this meeting other than the honor of making his acquaintance, when Langston straightened up.

"These all yours?" he queried mildly.

Kristin nodded, almost wishing she could deny ownership. Gray took a step closer, as if he'd felt the quailing tremors of uncertainty shaking Kristin and wanted to psychically shore her up.

"Hard to believe that someone as young as yourself could show such mastery of film photography. Film prints have an ineffable quality impossible to achieve digitally. They remind me of Ansel Adams's work. They're quite remarkable. At last, a fresh vision of the Sangre de Cristos."

Kristin had to do a lot of psychological backtracking to catch up with Harrell Langston's verdict. He liked her stuff? She turned to Gray to make sure that she hadn't hallucinated. He cocked an eyebrow in her direction as if to say, "I told you so," and Kristin knew it was true.

"Okay, now," Langston began, picking up a pencil and waving it through the air as if he were sketching out the work left to be done on his next exhibit. "This is going to be a five-, no, a six-artist show, counting you." He pointed the pencil eraser in Kristin's direction. "And then let's see, there will be Hughes, Spatoonak . . ." Kristin's head swam as Langston methodically reeled off the names. She'd never dreamed of being among such exalted company.

"So"—Langston concluded his calculations—"we should have room for about a dozen of your prints, Kristin. Think you can winnow them down to that number?"

"Happily," Kristin answered, trying to maintain a semblance of poise when she felt like prancing with joy like a frisky colt.

"Good. They'll all need to be reprinted." Langston

gave the order as if it had been expected, although it took Kristin completely by surprise. "May I suggest you use a German photographic paper that will give you that extra scintilla of luster the prints lack now?"

An extra scintilla of luster, Kristin thought. A moment before she had been proud of the quality of her prints. Now, looking through Harrell Langston's eyes, she saw quite clearly that they were slightly flat. Though reprinting would mean more long hours in the drafty, gasoline-smelling darkroom, she was grateful to Langston for applying his masterful eye to her work and discerning how it could be improved. It was an improvement that few would have seen and fewer would have felt was worth the trouble of making. Kristin began to fully appreciate why Harrell Langston was the best.

"We'll need the prints by the middle of this week. Will that create any difficulties for you?"

"None," Kristin murmured, wondering where on earth she was going to find the time. She had lessons scheduled all day long throughout the Christmas holidays. She'd find a way, though. If it meant seeing her work hang on the walls of the Langston Gallery, she'd most definitely find a way.

"How about lunch at Raul's?" Gray suggested as they stepped into the winter sunshine of the courtyard. "You look like a person who needs to either celebrate or burst."

"Is it that obvious?" Kristin asked, feeling as if she

were beaming high-wattage exultation like a lighthouse signaling to boats on a foggy sea. "I can't believe it," she whooped when they were out of earshot of the gallery. "Me. At the Langston Gallery. It's just not real."

"Of course it's real, babe. I told you he'd love your stuff."

Sharing it with Gray was as good as the moment of triumph itself had been. At Raul's, Kristin saw yet another side of Gray unfold—Gray the resort owner. It was funny that Kristin should see this side last, since it appeared to be the one that had made Gray a local celebrity.

"Good to see you again, Mr. Lowrey," the hostess greeted them at the door. On the short trip through the homey restaurant, Kristin began to get a slight feel for the power Gray wielded as the owner of a ski resort and one of the county's largest employers.

"Have you thought any more about the condominiums I suggested you put in up at Powderhorn?" a burly man in a western-cut suit asked Gray. "Sure would like to make some bids on the work," he added with what he probably hoped would be an ingratiating smile.

"Haven't quite made up my mind about it, Cal," Gray said, breaking away from the man's death-grip handshake with the finesse of a skilled politician.

"There'll be condominiums at my resorts," Gray whispered to Kristin as they stepped away from the man's table, "the same day they put up a tombstone with the name Grayson Lowrey on it. But I'd never tell Cal that. I'll just keep stalling him for the next fifty years. In a town this small, it doesn't pay to make enemies." No sooner had they turned to leave, however, than someone hailed him from the next table, a leading citizen trying to wangle a job for his ne'er-do-well son. At the next two tables other leading lights of Taos inquired after Gray's health and the condition of the snow.

"Powder Johnson and Johnson would kill for," Gray quipped.

"Hey," another voice called out, "heard that Amy St. Peters is coming back to Powderhorn for Christmas vacation again this year. Bring her to my New Year's Eve party. She seemed to enjoy it last time." The invitation was accompanied by a ribald gust of laughter that indicated it was Gray's company the famous actress had enjoyed more than the party.

"Thanks," Gray said noncommittally as he took Kristin by the elbow and steered her to their table.

"Amy St. Peters?" Kristin inquired, archly camouflaging a stab of jealousy behind her mocking tone.

"Yes, one of the truly great minds of the American cinema," Gray replied in the same joking vein. "We spent the evening discussing existentialism, the new Latin American literature, and the color of her nail polish. An evening I'll treasure. Now that we've finally made it to our table, may I suggest anything on the menu? Having tried it all, I can assure you that nothing comes out of Raul's kitchen unless it's good."

"That's quite a statement."

"Have I lied to you yet?" Gray asked, his eyes sparkling.

Kristin laughed, enjoying the camaraderie that had sprung up between them and wishing that she could erase the last traces of longing deep within her that cried out for more, far more. Gray had proved himself to be a good and generous friend, first by sheltering her from an involvement that he knew would lead to inevitable heartache and now, by making it possible for her work to hang on the walls of the Langston Gallery. *Why*, she wondered bitterly, *couldn't that be enough?* It would simply *have* to be, came the curt answer as she stifled her wayward regrets. She would be as good a friend to Gray as he had already been to her.

"How are the chiles rellenos?" Kristin inquired about her favorite Mexican food.

"You've never had the dish until you've tasted Raul's."

"That sounds like recommendation enough for me."

The green chilies stuffed with cheese and fried in a fluffy cornmeal batter were superb.

"Here, if you like those," Gray said, offering her a forkful of food cut from his own plate, "try some of the blue corn tortilla enchiladas."

"*Muy delicioso*," Kristin declared, after swallowing the tasty morsel. "Try some of the rellenos." As she slid her plate toward Gray, she tried to imagine someone like Dennis Hascomb exchanging tastes of his meal with her. In contrast to Gray's natural warmth, Dennis seemed stuffy, cold, and pretentious. *Of course*, came the unavoidable reminder, *Dennis wanted to marry you and this, a shared meal, is as far as you and Gray will ever go.*

"We'd better get back up the mountain," Gray announced, finishing off the last of the yeasty sopapillas dripping with honey. "Laurie will be waiting."

"That's right," Kristin agreed with sudden alarm. "I almost forgot—I have a class this afternoon."

Back at the lodge, Kristin's class was already gathered around the main fireplace awaiting her arrival when she showed up. Addie and Laurie intercepted them halfway across the hall.

"Gray, they've been calling you all morning from Powderhorn. The main chair lift is on the fritz and they can't locate the mechanic."

The carefree air that had lightened Gray's dark features during their outing to Taos was shadowed by a fresh layer of worry. "Call over there, Addie," he directed, "and tell them I'm on my way. I think I can locate the mechanic and I'll bring him with me. Contact Le Piste Rouge and have Chef Guillame send over a huge batch of hors d'oeuvres, wine, and coffee to anyone waiting in a lift line."

"Daddy." A small voice called for his attention next. "Where have you been? It's Christmas. Are you going to pull me on the sled now?"

Guilt slithered over Kristin for having taken Laurie's father from her on Christmas Day.

Gray kneeled down to address the little girl. "Listen, Button, there's a big emergency over at the other ski place and I'm going to have to be gone for a while."

Kristin watched the usually merry eyes flood with tears of disappointment and she quickly bent down to speak in a soft voice to the unhappy child.

"Laurie, maybe you'd like to come with me and Punkin'. We're going to teach a ski class now and you could help us."

"Me and Punkin'?" Laurie asked, tentatively investigating the offer, her head tilted upward to Kristin.

"That's right."

Laurie looked from Kristin to her father, then over to Punkin' collapsed on her favorite rug in front of the fire. The tears receded. "That would be okay," she decided.

Gray caught Kristin's eye above Laurie's head. "Her heart," he reminded her in a whisper.

"I'll keep her with me," Kristin assured him. "You'd better go find that mechanic," she added for Laurie's benefit, "or there will be a lot of unhappy people who came a long way to ski."

Gray's pat on her arm as he left was for a trusted friend. Kristin just wished she could truly feel like one.

Kristin went through her introduction-to-cross-country-skiing lecture with the class gathered around her by the fire and Laurie settled contentedly in her lap. Kristin found she liked the feel of the small body nestled against her own, liked it when Laurie turned to her with a spontaneous smile that said the feeling was mutual.

Outside in the pasture, Kristin sat Laurie on a stump in a sunny patch while she led the class through the basic maneuvers. After several demonstrations and some practice exercises, Kristin had her students circle around her as they made their first awkward attempts at cross-country skiing.

"Glide," she coached a trim middle-aged woman. "Left hand forward, right ski back," she shouted to a rotund businessman. "Good form, Edgar," she complimented a wiry elderly man. Kristin was concentrating so hard on her class's progress that she was startled when she felt a small hand tug on her pants.

"I want to ski too," Laurie asserted, her slanted eyes serious.

"Laurie, honey, you should be watching."

"But I want to ski with everybody else. I can do it. I

know I can," Laurie protested with a heart-tugging earnestness.

"But we don't have skis small enough for you," Kristin explained. It was the truth; there was no equipment Laurie's size at High Country. But the larger truth was that Laurie's malformed heart would never allow her to attempt such a vigorous sport.

"But I really want to," Laurie said patiently. Kristin could tell that she was struggling to swallow back the tears that were welling in her eyes.

"Here, Laurie," Kristin said, suddenly inspired, "why don't you put your feet on top of my skis?" She lifted the little girl up so that she had one foot on the top of each of Kristin's skis. "Okay now, lift up your foot," Kristin instructed, then she pushed forward. They glided together for a few feet and Laurie cackled with excited laughter.

"Ski some more," she cried out, and Kristin pushed off again. Soon her class had stopped practicing and they were all watching the tandem ski demonstration.

"Hey, Laurie, you look like a pro." Eric passed by the pasture leading a group he'd taken out early that morning.

"I'm skiing, Eric," Laurie called out.

"Come on," Kristin said, scooping Laurie into her arms, "Punkin' is getting lonely." Kristin's class broke into applause as she carried Laurie back to the stump where Punkin' waited. Laurie smiled her impish grin and waved at the students like a miniature Rose Bowl queen.

Kristin couldn't suppress an amused chuckle. "You little character," she whispered to Laurie.

Just as the class was ending, Eric reappeared, carrying an old pair of skis that had been discarded from the rental shop.

"A cross-country ski built for two," he announced, presenting the skis with a flourish.

"Eric, you're a genius," Kristin burst out as she saw the tiny bindings mounted in front of the regular ones on the battered skis and understood what they were for.

Hiding his embarrassment behind a display of theatrical sheepishness complete with digging his toe in the snow and an "Aw, shucks, ma'am," Eric held out a pair of poles sized to fit the bindings. Kristin hurriedly unpopped the bindings on her regular pair of skis and attached her ski boots to the pair Eric had modified.

"Come on, Laurie," Kristin announced, approaching the stump, "now we can really do some skiing." She placed the smaller feet in front of her own and clamped Laurie's shoes down. "And here are your poles."

"Awesome," the little girl whispered. They pushed off. Kristin could extend her leg to kick them forward only a fraction of the usual distance, but it was more than enough to give Laurie the ride of her lifetime.

"Look at me, Daddy. I'm skiing!"

Kristin jerked her head up. She had been so absorbed

in watching the measured steps she was forced to take to accommodate Laurie's short legs that she hadn't seen Gray approach.

"You sure are, sweetheart," he called back to his daughter, watching the awkward, sliding steps Kristin was making. "That's enough now," he announced a few minutes later. "You don't want to get too tired out." Gray advanced toward them and kneeled in the snow to release the set of child-sized bindings Eric had rigged up. Once she was free, Gray swept Laurie into his arms.

"That was more fun than anything, Daddy," Laurie bubbled over.

Kristin took joy in seeing Laurie's face, ruddy with exercise, beaming next to her father's.

"Can I ski some more tomorrow?" she asked as the three of them headed for the lodge.

"Kristin is going to be awfully busy for the next week," Gray answered.

"You can ski with me, can't you, Kristin?" Laurie asked imploringly.

"I *am* going to be busy," Kristin cautioned, "but I think we can probably squeeze in a few ski outings."

"You're nice. Do you have a little girl?" The need in Laurie's question spoke straight to Kristin's heart. She shook her head in a negative answer. "She's nice, isn't she, Daddy?"

“Yes, quite nice.” The icy chill in Gray’s tone froze the tide of emotion rising in Kristin, directly contradicting his words. “Laurie, you’d better not bother Kristin anymore while you’re here on vacation. She has to teach ski classes and get ready for an important art show, so she’s not going to have any time to spend with you.”

“Daddy . . .” A defeated whimper was Laurie’s only protest, but Kristin knew the interdict had been directed at her. In no uncertain terms, Grayson Lowrey had just ordered her to stay away from his child.

Chapter 9

K*ristin was thankful that the* next week was a busy one. Between her lessons and the slow drives down the mountain for long sessions of reprinting in her rented darkroom, she had no time to dwell on Gray's latest rebuff. It was there, in the darkroom, that she found consolation—seeing what Harrell Langston had called "that extra scintilla of luster" emerge in her new prints. With developing solution dripping off her elbows, Kristin held up the latest photo she was reprinting—the infrared rendition of the icicle-hung stream. On the new paper that Langston had recommended, the thin trickle of water now seemed fifty feet deep, such was the richness of the revised print. Kristin literally had to drag herself away from the photo to continue work on the negatives still remaining to be redone. She dumped out all the chemical baths and set up new ones for color work, then located the negative she'd shot of the alpenglow.

The reddish-lavender shimmering across the snow acquired a golden patina when Kristin reprinted it on the new paper. That golden haze lent the ephemeral image an illusion of permanence. *Permanence, what a cruel joke.* The thought darted across Kristin's brain before she could consciously extinguish it, triggering the one memory she fought to suppress, the memory of her and Gray and the few moments they'd shared. Moments that had turned out to be as brief and impermanent as alpenglow. Irritated at herself for such a futile and undisciplined line of thinking, Kristin forcefully focused on keeping track of the precise number of seconds the print had to slosh around in each of the chemical baths.

The day had been long. Earlier that afternoon, she'd instructed a particularly ungainly group. It had taken her nearly two hours longer than normal to deliver on her promise that everyone in that class would be skiing by the end of the afternoon. The trees were casting long shadows by the time she finally had her last student gliding across the snow. She'd skipped dinner, a habit she'd acquired since her last confrontation with Gray. Kristin was just as eager to avoid Gray during his holiday stay at High Country as he was to shield Laurie from any further contact with her.

As she tipped the fix bath from side to side, rolling miniature waves over the alpenglow photo, she had to admit that she could understand why Gray had done what he had. He didn't want Laurie to form an attachment to someone who would inevitably leave. She understood how terribly Laurie had been hurt before when her own mother had abandoned her. Still, Kristin thought, letting the chemical waves lap higher and higher up the sides of the tray, still Gray didn't have to be so brusque, so infernally hurtful.

She slid the print into the washer and watched as the apparatus bubbled water over the mauve-tinted snowscape until it looked like a scene from a snowy underwater kingdom she once might have visited in a dream. Abruptly she turned up the pressure on the water faucet, feeding the washer until the print was lost beneath an angry spray of bubbles. Weary as she was, Kristin looked through her files for yet another negative. She had to finish at least one more print tonight if she was going to be ready for the opening on New Year's Eve.

The drive home over the tortuous roads seemed endless. Kristin stumbled into bed without even bothering to undress. Reeking of chemicals and ignoring the growls from her empty stomach, she abandoned herself to the profound sleep of the utterly exhausted.

Minutes later, or so it seemed to Kristin, she awoke to the feel of bright sunlight striping her face as it streamed in through the curtains around her window. For a moment she simply lay in bed, leisurely stretching the infinite number of sore muscles protesting their overuse. Then, in one burst of motion, Kristin sprang out of bed. If the sun was high enough to peek in her window, she was late for her morning class. She skipped across the cold floor to the window and threw back the curtain.

A class of obvious beginners was following the well-worn circular tracks around the perimeter of the pasture. Like a hub on a rotating wheel directing the motion, Gray was at their center. He had taken her class. She stripped off the clothes she'd fallen asleep in and, after a quick shower in the frigid bathroom, tugged on a pair of jeans, a turtleneck, and a hand-knit wool cardigan from Iceland. The sweater was Kristin's favorite, with its bold geometric pattern in browns and tans and its buttons of patterned silver.

"Whoa, there," Addie called out as Kristin headed full steam through the main hall.

"Sorry, I can't stop now," Kristin apologized. "I overslept and Gray's got my class out there. I've got to go and relieve him."

"You'll do no such thing," Addie said firmly. "The boss left orders that you were to be allowed to sleep in as long as you liked, then fed a glutton's breakfast, and I never disobey the boss," Addie warned ominously before breaking into a grin. "So get on out to the kitchen and place your order." Brandishing a spatula, she herded Kristin away from the door.

The clatter of skis being dragged across the floor of the main hall alerted Kristin that the lesson had ended. She was sipping the last of her coffee and quickly rose to leave, wanting to fade away before Gray appeared.

"Mind if I join you?" Gray stood at the kitchen door, blocking her planned retreat.

Kristin was caught off balance by his unexpected appearance and, as always, by his sheer physical mass. The doorframe seemed exactly that, a frame that Gray's broad shoulders and long, muscled legs filled to near capacity. "It's your lodge," Kristin replied, attempting a lighthearted flippancy that fell flat.

"Well, I've played short-order cook long enough," Addie said, sensing the strain in the atmosphere. "I'd better tend to my bookwork upstairs." She slid past Gray, who paid her the briefest of attentions; his gaze was locked on Kristin.

"Beautiful sweater," he commented after Addie had left the two of them alone together. His eyes traveled across the swell of her breasts beneath the unbuttoned cardigan, letting Kristin know that his remark covered much more than her sweater. Abruptly he turned away, as if annoyed with himself for allowing his eyes to stray to such provocative territory; he poured a cup of coffee. Pivoting, he held the pot up toward Kristin. "More?"

She nodded her acceptance; it would be more awkward now to retreat than it would be to stay. As he refilled her cup, Kristin noticed how the back of his hand, on the side opposite his thumb, was tufted with dark hair. She wondered if his chest was covered with the same springy mat. Against her will, a flash of an image appeared in her mind: her, lying nearly naked, caught in dying flickers of light from the office fireplace. Gray had seen her in most intimate detail while she had never so much as glimpsed him with his shirt off. She didn't even know whether he had hair on his chest. Something about that inequity struck her with an unexpected poignancy.

"You certainly do make it hard for a person to stay mad at you," Kristin said, trying to banish the dangerous thoughts.

Gray took a seat opposite her at the table. A tilt of his head indicated his confusion.

Kristin, wishing that, just once, she could have censored her natural candor, explained. "I mean, that was awfully nice of you to take my class this morning and let me sleep in."

"Were you mad at me?" Gray inquired gently.

"A little," she admitted, minimizing her feelings.

"Because of the way I reacted to you skiing with

Laurie?" he asked, already knowing the answer. "Surely you understand what I was doing. It would just be a guaranteed heartbreak if I let Laurie become attached to you. Although I think it's happened already. She was crying this morning when she left because I wouldn't let her wake you up to say good-bye."

"Good-bye?" A stab of panic took Kristin by surprise. "I thought Laurie was going to spend her Christmas holiday here. She shouldn't have gone back to Santa Fe for at least another week."

"She didn't; Betsy took her down to catch a flight for the West Coast. Her mother's been after me for a year to send Laurie out, but I've always resisted her attempts to reestablish contact. Seeing her with you the other day, the way she asked if you had a little girl, made me realize how selfish I'd been. Laurie needs to feel like she has a mother. And, although Jan is no maternal prizewinner, she's the only one Laurie's got."

Gray's expression of unwilling resignation told Kristin that the decision to send Laurie to visit with his ex-wife had come at a great psychic cost to him.

"You did the right thing." She comforted Gray with a pat on his hand, happy that, for once, she truly did feel like a friend to him. Before the touch could be prolonged into anything that would rip the thin veneer from Kristin's feelings and expose what she knew lurked beneath, she withdrew her hand.

"I'd better go check and see how many are registered for the afternoon class."

"Don't bother," Gray ordered. "I'm taking that class too. You only have two days until the show opens and I'll bet you still haven't talked to Harrell about mounting and framing your prints."

"My gosh," Kristin blurted out. "I'd focused so much on just getting all the prints done that I'd completely ignored all of that."

"You'd better get into town, woman," Gray commanded teasingly, "before Harrell has to tack your work to the wall."

"There it is," Harrell Langston declared, holding one of Kristin's prints out in front of him. "I knew that depth, that luster, was there, and you've brought it out. How did you like that paper I recommended?"

"That's what made the difference," Kristin said, swallowing the idiot's grin that was blooming on her face in response to Langston's unabashed praise. "That, and I played around a little with the exposure times."

"Takes some experimentation, doesn't it?" Langston said, gently laying the print down. "Weston James once told me that his avocado and tin kitchen funnel print—you know the one I'm talking about?" Langston asked, scraping some stray wisps of long silver hair out of his face and fastening them back with his ponytail.

"Of course," Kristin murmured at the reference to a print she'd seen reproduced in every photography text she'd ever picked up.

"Anyway, James told me that he made a hundred and twenty-seven different versions of that print until he got the damned thing right. Perfectionism, Kristin," Langston intoned, "that's the name of the game. Nothing less than your finest. Now, let's see about mounting your finest." He led the way into a back room where Kristin was surprised to discover a cottage industry in full swing—the framing and mounting rooms of the Langston Gallery.

"Take your pick," Langston said, offering Kristin her choice of a dozen different shades of gray mounting board for her black and whites. She indicated a dark-charcoal one.

"Good." Langston confirmed her selection. "With the richness of the blacks in your infrareds, you'll need something that dark. And now for the color prints."

The choices of mounting board available to back her color work were mind-boggling. After long deliberation, she settled on a blue as deep and vibrant as a New Mexico sky. Langston approved that choice as well. They stood back in silence and watched as Langston's professional framers went to work measuring and cutting the board.

"Have you known Gray long?" Langston asked.

The casual question caught Kristin unaware. For a second she was afraid that her feelings for her employer must have been obvious to Langston, but one glance at his face told Kristin that the question had been intended simply to make conversation.

"No, actually I just met him when I came to High Country to apply for a job. How about yourself, have you known him long?"

"Practically from the day he set foot in town. He's always been what I call a born art lover. That's someone who gravitates toward galleries through an inborn love of art. He's not the typical gallery crawler who shows up at an opening to see and be seen. Anyway, he stumbled in here not long after he arrived and we started skiing together. He introduced me to cross-country after both of us got fed up with the long lift lines. We've been a bit out of touch recently; how's he doing? I mean with his daughter and that whole situation."

"Fine," Kristin answered, not knowing how much she should divulge. "Laurie's out in California now, visiting her mother for a few days."

Langston nodded pensively. "Never knew a man who cared so much about his child," he muttered. "It was almost as if he felt personally responsible for the child's infirmity."

"What do you mean?" Kristin asked, trying not to let the urgent curiosity she felt seep into her voice.

"I don't quite know," Langston replied. "It's more a feeling I have that a lot of strong guilt is mixed up with the even stronger love he has for Laurie. I can't really explain it. I do know this, though: Lowrey is probably, in addition to being the physically largest man I know and one of the most powerful, also one of the kindest. He'd throttle me for saying that," Langston chuckled, "but it's true. An unusual combination, don't you think?"

"I really can't say I know Gray that well," Kristin lied. She was afraid that if she spoke her heart, agreeing with Langston and dwelling on all Grayson Lowrey's sterling qualities, she would end the conversation choking back tears. "I guess I'd better retire to the darkroom for the rest of the day. I still have several negatives left to reprint."

"Do get them to me as soon as you can," Langston cautioned. "We're already pushing it a bit as it is. One last thing," he added, walking Kristin to the door. "Of course, you're free to invite anyone you want to the opening. We had just enough time to include you on the invitation we sent out for the opening-night reception. I sent several down to Albuquerque, to some of the galleries there that deal in photography and to the art critic—what's her name?"

"Felicia Cliver." Kristin supplied the missing name. Her mouth had gone suddenly dry. Would the vituperative critic unmask her? Harrell hadn't actually asked if she'd ever exhibited before, but Kristin certainly hadn't volunteered the information.

“Right. Anyway, I thought you’d appreciate the exposure in the hometown press.”

“Thanks,” Kristin murmured in response to Harrell’s well-meant intentions. There was no enthusiasm in her voice, however, because the prospect of meeting the woman who had publicly crucified her held little joy for Kristin. She imagined Gray reading the critic’s acid evaluation of her work and winced inwardly. In a flash she realized that the fantasy behind all her work and hopes for this show was that Gray would see her as a talented, respected artist and would rescind his ban on emotional involvement. Deep within the illogical heart of her being, a heart that drove her as strongly as Gray’s drove him, Kristin was dreaming that her success would make Gray love her. Feeling like a sham, she bid Harrell a hasty good-bye and retreated to her sanctuary, the darkroom.

Chapter 10

New Year's Eve did not herald the beginning of a fresh year; it meant opening night to Kristin. She'd finished the last print late the night before and, using the spare key Harrell had loaned her, had dropped it off at the gallery to be mounted and framed.

The sensation of walking into the empty gallery late at night had been an eerie one. When she'd come face-to-face with a wallful of her prints, she'd had the unsettling feeling of catching an unexpected glimpse of herself in a store window. Just as she sometimes made an instantaneous evaluation of the image, thinking, *Now there's an attractive woman*, before she realized it was herself she was staring at, Kristin reacted reflexively to the wall of prints. *They're good*, she thought, taking in at a glance the whole sweep of them. On the heels of that lightning-quick appraisal came the awareness, *They're mine.*

Kristin had stepped back and, in the quiet of the

deserted gallery, studied her work. *They hang together*, she had thought, looking at the individual prints as pieces of a larger assemblage. Together they formed a cohesive whole. The effect pleased her and soothed her rising anxiety about the possibility of Felicia Cliver putting in an appearance. Still, Kristin had reminded herself, she'd been confident about her Albuquerque show before it opened. That remembrance had wedged a crack large enough in her confidence to allow the black crows of doubt enough room to reenter and come home to roost. She'd dropped off the print and left.

Those winged harbingers of doubt still seemed to be hovering about her the morning of the show. With a mental wave of her arm, she put the ominous birds to flight and shrugged the covers off. By Gray's decree, there was to be no afternoon class, so she just had the morning session to worry about.

Her mind was not on her lesson that day. Fortunately, she was blessed with an unusually coordinated, easily instructed group that absorbed the principles of cross-country skiing almost intuitively.

As soon as the class broke up, Kristin rushed upstairs. She'd lighted the small space heater in the bathroom before leaving and the room was toasty. For the first time since she'd arrived, she filled the tub and luxuriated in a long soak. As she soaked, she tried to empty her mind of confusion, doubts, and false hopes. She wanted to arrive at her opening unencumbered by such burdensome excess baggage. Try as she might, however, she couldn't root out the image of Gray, warmed by the glow of her success, enfolding her in his arms.

Thoroughly irritated at herself for being unable to dash such futile hopes, Kristin ripped the plug out of the tub. The bathwater drained away, quickly swirling out in an ever-widening whirlpool. Her irritation increased when she confronted her wardrobe and realized that, in her frenzy of preparation, she had neglected her own personal presentation. She had nothing to wear. Nothing, at any rate, that was suitable for an artist's opening night. Once again she was stuck with her old standby nice jeans and black cashmere sweater combo. She was going to look like an applicant for a clerical job instead of a trendsetting, bohemian artist. Having little else to work with, Kristin concentrated on adding a note of drama to her appearance by hauling out her cache of rarely used cosmetics and revamping her face.

Her full mouth bloomed even more lushly beneath a coating of peach gloss. Outlined in a smoky green, her eyes truly did resemble chunks of Cerrillos turquoise. After weeks in the sun, her apricot-toned skin didn't need its color heightened, but a touch of blusher emphasized her high cheekbones. She whirled her long auburn tresses into a thick twist of hair that she pinned atop her head. Wispy tendrils, still wet from her bath, curled at the nape of her gracefully arched neck.

Downstairs, Eric unleashed a low wolf whistle when she appeared.

"Oh, Eric," Kristin chided, "I thought you were above being fooled by a few dabs of war paint. It's still the same old Kristin underneath."

"False modesty," Betsy said, joining in the teasing. "But why are you ready so early?"

"I wanted to see if there were any last-minute details Harrell needed my help with."

"She's nervous," Eric observed to the group at large. "The artist is nervous on opening day. Happens all the time. What the nervous artist needs to do," he advised solemnly, "is to find a bar where the lighting is quite dim and the beer quite cold and just lay low until it's time for you to show up."

"I take it this is an all-purpose prescription," Kristin responded, enjoying the good-natured banter. "Good for nerves, heartbreaks, and the death of pet goldfish."

"Something like that," Eric grinned.

"Whose goldfish died?" Kristin recognized Gray's voice, although she would have sworn she sensed his presence as a tingling of the nerves at the base of her neck before she ever heard his voice.

"No one's goldfish died," Eric groaned. "I was just

telling Kristin that she should go out and get quietly bombed before her show."

"Not a bad suggestion," Gray agreed. "Want to take him up on it?"

Kristin ignored the way her body warmed as Gray approached. "Listen, you two chuckleheads," Kristin warned, "I'm going to be enough of a wreck already without being a paralytic drunk to boot."

"You're not wearing that, are you?" Gray asked, just noticing the jeans and sweater. Kristin responded with a blank look. "I mean tonight, to the opening?" Gray elaborated.

"I'd planned to, unless you think either my stretch jumpsuit or nightgown would be more appropriate, because those are practically my only other choices."

All hint of frivolity disappeared. Gray studied her like a business proposition he was taking under advisement. "I'm glad I came by. Come on, I know just where to take you to get you outfitted."

The complex stew of emotions that Gray stirred up bubbled too close to the surface. His presumptuous announcement caused those suppressed feelings to flare up in Kristin's response. "'Outfitted'?" Kristin repeated the term incredulously. "And just what gives you the right to make judgments on the way I choose to clothe myself and then to treat me like I'm some piece of furniture you want to have reupholstered?"

Kristin's flash of anger caused Eric and Betsy to discreetly fade away, leaving Kristin to face Gray alone beneath the vaulted ceiling of the main hall.

Gray didn't answer; his response was lost somewhere between the bottomless dazzlement of her eyes and the unbearable plumpness of her lips. Gray thought of those lips yielding beneath his own, parting to allow him access to the sweet bounty within. Like the foot of a furious giant, his conscious mind stomped on the wildfire of desire that had begun to smolder deep within him.

"Don't get all prickly," Gray commanded in a headlong flight from the arousal to which he forbade himself to surrender. "I know the Taos art community. Now, it's one thing to actually get into a show at Harrell Langston's gallery and to hear him praise your work. It's entirely another matter to sell that work, and, ultimately, that's what your success or failure rests upon."

His words were incontrovertible. He had, in a few succinct phrases, summed up the basic hard truth about making it in the art world, where the ultimate test of success was whether or not you sold.

When Gray saw that his harsh words were soaking in, he continued. "You should also know that it's a very rare gallery goer who truly knows what he or she likes, who has the confidence to purchase an artist's work with no knowledge of the artist or his or her reputation. That's not too difficult to understand, is it? You're making a personal statement with your photographs, Kristin; people want to know what the person behind the statement is like. I doubt that they're going to be terribly receptive when they discover that it is a shop clerk. Or someone who dresses like one, at any rate."

"Thank you most kindly for your critique," Kristin answered icily. "Now, if you will be so good as to get out of my way." As she started forward, a hand gripped her forearm. The pressure was light, but in the way the pressure of the ocean against bare skin is light. Kristin knew that an enormous strength waited, held in check behind the imprisoning grip.

"Don't go." Gray's tone had fewer shades of command in it and more of supplication. "It seems that I spend half my time with you apologizing and the other half doing something to offend you. I spoke too bluntly. What you have on is fine—for anything other than an art opening. I've been to hundreds of them. They're the principal source of amusement in Taos. All I wanted to say is that it would give me great pleasure to help you find something really extraordinary to wear tonight."

As always, Kristin couldn't resist the contrition in Gray's voice. The tension relaxed on the arm he held captive. Gray took the tiny slump as an encouraging sign.

"After all, you are my protégée. Naturally I want you to shine tonight."

"'Naturally,'" Kristin parroted, repeating the word

but giving it a wry twist. The restraining force of Gray's hand on her arm was transformed into something else entirely as she stopped struggling against it. A current pulsed between them that neutralized Kristin's hostility. She noticed a tiny dark triangle at the base of the V where Gray's camel-colored sweater opened. *He does have hair on his chest*, Kristin thought.

Once diverted onto this tormenting tangent, other disturbing thoughts followed. Even the awareness of the power in that deep chest, the arms ropy with muscle—a power that had been fleetingly manifested in his hold on her arm—excited Kristin. Standing beside so many men, she'd often felt gawky and oversized. Not with Gray. Next to him she was a delicate porcelain figurine. Something deep within her exalted at the feeling. Gray's hand fell away.

"So, you wouldn't be mortally offended if I took you to a little shop a friend of mine owns?"

"No, not mortally." Kristin noted that Gray sounded as if he'd had to hastily collect himself and his thoughts. It was a small comfort to learn that she was not alone in her turmoiled response to the brief contact.

The "little shop" contained a selection of clothes that seemed to have taken shape from Kristin's dreams, and the "friend" who owned it was a woman who blended sophistication and warmth in a way that few can.

"If you're opening at the Langston Gallery tonight,"

she said, echoing Gray's explanation of their visit, "we'd better find something worthy of the occasion." Her smile flickered from Kristin to Gray. As it settled on Gray, however, Kristin noticed that some of the sparkle went out of it. An instant later the boutique owner had revived her expression. But the woman's guard had been down long enough for Kristin to see clearly that her feelings for Gray went far beyond friendship. It was equally clear as Gray wandered off toward a rack of dresses that the feeling was not reciprocated. Kristin wondered if Taos was filled with women pining for the unattainable Grayson Lowrey and hiding their longing behind a facade of friendship. With an evil genius, jealousy needled a question into her: Have she and Gray slept together? Did he make it a practice to sleep with all his "friends" before declaring any further intimacy out of bounds?

"How's this?" Gray held up an outlandish outfit of hand-painted silk. Kristin stepped forward and fingered the sumptuous ivory silk painted with a pastel border done in a subtle abstract design. The material had been fashioned into a thigh-length kimono-style top and flowing harem pants. It was so different from anything Kristin even saw in the stores where she could afford to shop, much less had ever thought of owning, that she didn't know how to react for a second.

"It's gorgeous," she whispered at last as the silk undulated beneath her fingers.

"Try it on."

The shop owner looked to Kristin for confirmation. Kristin nodded her head. In the dressing-room mirror Kristin saw herself lifted out of the mundane and transplanted into the marvelous. She tightened the sash around her waist and saw a creature out of a fairy tale mimic her action. It was hard to believe that it was Kristin Jonsson inhabiting such fanciful clothes. The fabric skimmed over her body, draping across her curves to reveal them in ways they had never been revealed before. The caressing feel of the silk seduced Kristin, drawing her into the spell it cast.

"Does it fit?" Gray's question summoned her forth. Trapped in the fantasy woven by the storybook apparel, Kristin felt like a geisha about to be presented to the ruling shogun, a harem girl summoned by the sultan to seek his approval.

"*Now* you look like an artist." Gray passed judgment on the ensemble. "Someone capable of bringing magic into ordinary lives."

Kristin was delighted by Gray's description of the artist. It put into words what she had always instinctively felt about the role of art in everyday life and the artist as a bearer of magic.

"There's just one thing missing," he said, unbuckling his belt and threading it out through the loops of his jeans. "Take off your sash."

Curiosity forced Kristin to obey. She held out the sash with one hand and clutched the front of the kimono together with the other.

Gray slid several conchos, fashioned of silver cast into embellished ovals and set with turquoise, off his belt. When Gray had threaded half a dozen onto the sash, he looped it around Kristin's waist and bound it there.

"Great effect," he said, stepping back to view his handiwork. "That gives you just the right southwestern touch without your having to dress up like Pocahontas. It also sets off your necklace nicely." Kristin's hand went to her throat. She'd forgotten that Gray's gift had been exposed by the plunging cut of the ivory silk top. "Well, what do you think?" he asked. "Should we clip off the tags?"

Kristin glanced briefly at the shop owner while Gray waited for Kristin's verdict. Jealousy and resignation swam in the woman's gaze, as if she knew in advance that there was no point in her feeling possessive of what she could never have. Kristin realized that the woman assumed that she and Gray were lovers, that the clothes were a lover's present. She wished she could telepathically communicate to the woman the knowledge that she and Gray were also "just friends." That the intimacy she was jealous of didn't exist between them. Suddenly Kristin wanted to leave, to escape from the reminder of the pain, the futile longing, that was so much like her own.

"It's lovely," Kristin muttered.

"Good, then it's settled. What about a wrap? It's freezing outside."

"No, that's fine," she mumbled, wanting very much to leave. "I have my parka. I can wear that over to the gallery; no one will see me in it."

"Have it your way." Gray shrugged. He turned to the shop owner and arranged to have the bill sent to him at his office at Powderhorn.

As they walked outside, Kristin faced him squarely. "I'll pay you back in installments," she said firmly.

A shadow crossed Gray's face. "Kristin, I told you it would give me pleasure to do this. Don't deny me this one small gesture of friendship."

"Friends do not buy one another silk evening wear. I appreciate what you've done, but I really must insist on repaying you."

Gray rolled his eyes heavenward as if seeking divine help in controlling his temper, which was threatening to erupt at the maddeningly obstinate woman beside him. "If that's what you want," Gray finally said, surrendering to Kristin's wishes. They walked the rest of the way in silence, each of them occupied with his or her own thoughts.

"Great, you're early," Harrell Langston boomed out when they walked in. The gallery was toasty warm and redolent with the spicy smell of a pot of mulled wine burbling off in a corner. Kristin shrugged off her parka. "Oh, that is really perfect," Harrell exclaimed, glimpsing Kristin's ivory silk outfit.

"Thank you," Kristin began, her voice still stiff from her quarrel with Gray. "Gray—"

"Kristin's eye for clothes is as sharp as her eye for photography." Gray cut in with a look to Kristin that warned her to let him generously give her credit for the spectacular outfit. Once again Kristin felt she was on an emotional seesaw, her feelings about Grayson Lowrey bouncing up and down with a rattling abruptness.

"All right, now, I'm going to put both of you to work. Gray can do the messy, heavy stuff and Kristin can handle all the more dainty chores. First off, Gray, I need you to haul in those pedestals that are back in the framing room. I had a couple of freestanding exhibits come in late this afternoon. And you, Miss Jonsson, if you'll be so good as to arrange the empanadas that Shirley made on the trays that are stacked out in the kitchen, maybe we'll have a chance at getting this opening off the ground."

By seven that evening, Kristin had arranged a dozen trays of hors d'oeuvres and set the five refreshment tables scattered throughout the gallery with holiday plates, cups, and centerpieces made from fiery red chilies and pine boughs. She'd also assisted Harrell in redirecting the lights on several of the oil paintings that were being displayed, helped him rehang two of her prints, vacuumed up the wood shavings that spilled from some newly framed pieces, and polished the glass on half a dozen smudged pieces. Just before he disappeared into the back of the gallery where he lived, Harrell popped open one of the innumerable bottles of champagne he had cooling.

"To your debut," he toasted Kristin. She and Gray hoisted their fluted glasses. "I'm not going to wish you good luck, because with your talent that would amount to an embarrassment of riches." He turned to Gray. "Thank you for bringing her to me." The three glasses clinked together.

The bubbles made a cheerful riot in Kristin's throat. A bang on the door alerted them that the other artists were arriving. Harrell hastily retired his glass and fled for the shower. "Be back in five minutes," he promised. "Don't let all the artists and their friends drink up all the bubbly. Save some for the paying customers."

Kristin answered the door, letting in the other artists in the show. As introductions were being made, Kristin sensed their nervousness, although they were all established artists. Her own apprehensions returned. Unlike the others in the show, she was far from established and had a great deal more to fear. She felt the fraudulence of having toasted to a "debut" a moment earlier and wished she had confessed the dismal failure of her real debut in Albuquerque. *Don't let Felicia Cliver come*, Kristin prayed. Almost imperceptibly at first, people trickled in, most arriving in clumps of two or three, with an occasional, more raucous, larger crowd filling the room.

"What's your medium?" asked a woman, dressed, as Gray would have said, like Pocahontas, with knee-high boots and a fringed skirt.

"Medium?" Kristin babbled as if she'd never heard the word before. The question had caught her in the middle of worrying about whether she could live through the experience of having Felicia Cliver savage her in print again. "Uh, photography. Film, not digital. These are mine here." She indicated the wall where her work hung.

The woman bobbed her head. "Nice. Quite nice. They're all yours?" she asked, looking from Kristin to the prints as if trying to reconcile the creation with the creator.

"Yes."

"I'm going to get Arturo. He'll really appreciate these." The woman hurried off, leaving Kristin to wonder if she could possibly mean Arturo Ramirez, one of the leaders of what was referred to as the New Taos School. Before Kristin had the answer to her question, a chilly wind blew in carrying Eric, Betsy, and Addie along with it.

"How's the nervous artist doing?" Eric asked, giving her a bolstering hug.

"Nervous," Kristin answered.

"Is this all your stuff?" Addie asked, goggle-eyed.

"Can't blame it on anyone else," Kristin joked.

"All framed like that, they look like something in a museum." Eric, Betsy, and Kristin broke into giggles at the reverence in Addie's voice. The older woman was momentarily miffed, then joined in, surrendering to their good-natured amusement.

"Oh, Punkin' says to give you her best wishes," Eric said. "She's sorry she couldn't make it, but they're showing *Rin Tin Tin* reruns tonight and she's always had a thing for hairy Germans. She said you'd understand."

"Eric," Betsy groaned.

Harrell Langston approached looking dapper in a suit of tan worsted wool set off by a cranberry silk tie. "This is my official gallery-owner costume," he explained, tightening the knot in the tie. Kristin introduced her friends.

"It's great to have your friends here to support you," Harrell cautioned with a smile, "but you're going to have to mix and mingle, you understand."

Before Kristin could respond, Harrell turned and addressed someone behind Kristin. "Felicia, darling, I'm so pleased you could make it. How was the drive up from Albuquerque? I hope the roads weren't too awful."

Kristin's stomach did a lurching flip-flop. She wanted to run, to disappear, to let the earth swallow her up, but she stayed rooted to the spot, unable to move. Worse still, she saw Gray emerge from the framing room where he'd been handling some last-minute details. *Go away*—she sent out urgent thought messages. But his long, loose strides continued to gobble up the space between them. At the same time, Harrell and a woman dressed entirely in black with a flamenco dancer's hat perched theatrically on her head converged upon her.

"Kristin," Harrell said, guiding the woman on his arm up to Kristin's circle, "I'd like you to meet Felicia Cliver, art critic for the Albuquerque paper. Felicia, this is Kristin Jonsson, my find of the season."

"I believe"—Felicia Cliver intoned the words dramatically—"that I am already familiar with Miss Jonsson's work. Didn't you have a show at Alana Moorington's gallery?"

Kristin looked into a pair of eyes as hard and flat and black as a snake's. Felicia Cliver knew full well the answer to her question before she'd ever asked it. In that instant, Kristin saw that the woman would have no scruples about sharing her opinion of Kristin Jonsson's work; she might even relish the experience of pillorying a budding artist in public simply for the shock value and to enhance her reputation as a mercilessly honest reviewer.

Not in front of Gray. The forlorn wish beat fervently through Kristin's mind as the critic eyed her work without really seeing it, just the way a cat doesn't really see a mouse—it sees only its next meal.

"I wanted you to have a chance to look over Kristin's

work," Harrell said, "because it shows an amazing depth for someone as young as she is."

"And how old are you, my dear?" Felicia purred. "Eighteen? Nineteen?"

Everyone laughed, assuming the comment to be a backhanded compliment on Kristin's youth. Kristin knew it wasn't. It was the first volley in the ruthless critic's attack. Even Harrell Langston's support would not save her from it. Gray moved closer to Kristin. She almost thought that he too had interpreted the true meaning of Felicia Cliver's remark and wanted to be beside Kristin to support her.

"You're doing pretty much the same sort of thing you were back in Albuquerque, aren't you?" Felicia Cliver asked Kristin, never taking her eyes off of the line of prints.

Kristin withered inside. The battle had been engaged. It would make no difference how she responded to the question. Felicia Cliver had disliked the photography in Kristin's first show and she had let the world know about it. The woman was intent upon doing the same thing tonight. Kristin thought of suddenly claiming a headache, appendicitis, anything to whisk Gray away so that he wouldn't hear the wounding words that were about to begin.

"As I said in Albuquerque—" the black-draped critic began. But before she could utter another word, she was cut off.

"Here's the stuff I was telling you about," the woman in the Pocahontas fringe bellowed out. She had a stocky Chicano man in tow. One look at his face, ennobled by a rich blend of Spanish and Native American blood, and Kristin knew that this was *the* Arturo Ramirez, the renowned painter. Even Felicia Cliver fell silent at his approach. "It's really different, isn't it?" The woman at his side chattered like a magpie. In contrast, Ramirez seemed as silent as a Mayan stone god.

He slipped away from the woman's grasp and advanced toward Kristin's prints, wearing the bedazzled expression of a pilgrim who has traveled hundreds of arduous miles and finally arrived at the shrine that is the object of his devotion. He ignored the pale, beringed hand that Felicia Cliver held out to him and devoted himself to Kristin's work, soaking it up through intense eyes.

"Whose are these?" he finally asked, turning to the silent group.

"Mine," Kristin volunteered in a squeaky voice.

"But you are so young," he said with his characteristic directness. "You must have old eyes to have seen what is in these photographs." He turned away, returning his scrutiny to the prints, not caring what the response to his pronouncement had been.

"Do you have a permanent darkroom?" Ramirez asked.

"I'm renting one."

"The reason I ask is because I've gotten together a cooperative studio. Our work as artists is such a solitary endeavor, is it not? It is easy to get lonely, so I like working with a group that can share ideas, enthusiasm. Anyway, we have a vacancy now in our darkroom. So few young photographers have mastered the art of printing the way you have. It's all just fast and digital. If you'd be interested, you could come by, meet the other artists, and see if you'd like working in our space."

On the outer edge of her peripheral vision, Kristin saw Felicia Cliver's mouth drop open. Though Kristin caught her own jaw before it swung slackly open in amazement, she had the same reaction—Arturo Ramirez was inviting her to join the New Taos School.

"You don't have to answer now," Ramirez interjected. "Think about it and let me know what you decide. Harrell can give you my address." With that, the legendary artist raised a hand in a truncated farewell and departed.

"Arturo never stays long," Harrell commented. "He comes to look at the new work, then leaves."

The observation went right by Kristin; she was lost in the euphoria of knowing Gray had been right there beside her to hear Arturo Ramirez's words.

"As you were saying, Felicia . . ." Harrell prompted the critic whose evaluation had been interrupted. "Something about what you had said in Albuquerque regarding Kristin's work."

"Oh, Harrell." Felicia Cliver's laugh came out a shrill cackle that made Kristin think of the black crows of doubt that had haunted her. "You know a good critic views an artist's work with a fresh perspective each time. I'd completely erased anything I'd ever thought or said about this very talented young photographer's work the minute I stepped into your gallery this evening."

"How extraordinarily wise of you," Harrell Langston soothed. "And what is your opinion now?"

"It would be a bit premature of me to say, wouldn't it? I mean, before my review is published."

Kristin had to confess to a certain small pleasure at watching the woman who had caused her such torment squirm under Harrell's questioning.

"Surely you can give us a small preview," Harrell urged.

"Harrell, darling," Felicia Cliver gushed, regaining her momentarily scattered poise, "do you ever show anything in your gallery that isn't utterly superb?"

"Never, Felicia," Harrell concurred. "I just wanted to be sure that you were fully aware of that fact."

"If you will excuse me," the critic said, kissing the air around Harrell's ears, "I must be pushing on. I have an absolute gauntlet of parties that I've promised to drop in on." She sighed with exasperation, as if she'd committed herself to the most odious of tasks.

All of Kristin's nervousness vanished when the critic

departed, and the opening became the best party she had ever attended. She looked around and saw that the gallery had come alive with throngs of artists, patrons, and friends of both. Waiters were circulating, pressing glasses of champagne on all-too-willing recipients. Chattering, nibbling clusters were grouped around each of the refreshment tables. Loud outbursts of greeting sounded, followed by hugs and airy kisses as new arrivals entered.

All around her, Kristin saw the proof of Gray's observation that a good part of the Taos populace was dedicated to displaying its outrageousness through its dress. The opening was starting to look like a costume party, complete with turn-of-the-century cowboys in knee-high boots and spurs, Pueblo Indians in ceremonially wrapped blankets, Parisian hookers in black berets and Cupid's bow lips, gypsies in a proliferation of fringed shawls and hoop earrings, and an assortment of Mexican peasants in brightly embroidered cottons. There was even a Goth-inspired contingent in black lipstick and matching black nail polish. The human canvas was far too arresting to allow most of the merrymakers to pay much attention to the painted ones hanging on the wall.

In the midst of the vividly entertaining tumult, Kristin felt calm and sure of herself with Gray by her side. He knew everyone in Taos's art community and introduced them all as they trickled past, charmed by Kristin's photography. He spoke for her, saying all the things that she never could have said herself.

"Now, Jack," he confided to a lawyer friend as the two of them stood in front of the infrared photo of the icy stream, "you're an outdoors guy like myself, so you'll appreciate this. Kristin skied in to a spot that *I* hadn't even known of to get this shot. Isn't it incredible? I mean, the way that stream looks like something from another planet or out of a dream. Don't you sometimes get that feeling when you're really off by yourself up in the mountains?"

The lawyer nodded his silent agreement. "Be right back," he blurted out a second later. Kristin watched as he buttonholed Harrell Langston. They returned and Harrell put an orange stick-on dot on the card describing the print. That dot signified that the work had been sold. Kristin turned to Gray in jubilation. He winked at her, then turned, his face deadpan, back to his friend to shake his hand and congratulate him on his fine taste.

"Cal"—Gray called out to the ruddy-faced contractor who had spoken to him at Raul's—"have you met Kristin Jonsson yet?"

The contractor held out a hand the size of a small ham for Kristin to shake.

"Can you believe these photographs, Cal? Look at this one." He directed the man's attention to a print of a stalk of wild grass glistening with hoarfrost. "Tell me, does Kitty have anything in that gem collection of hers to match this natural wonder?"

Kristin couldn't decide whether Cal eventually bought the print because he was struck by its beauty and wanted to make a gift of it to his wife, or because it was the financially expedient move to make, considering that the man who had strongly recommended its purchase also held the key to a multimillion-dollar construction project that his firm was avidly pursuing.

Kristin didn't have to wonder about the next two sales. Both were made to collectors who had nothing to gain by currying Gray's favor. Harrell shook his head in disbelief as he affixed yet another orange dot to the card beneath one of Kristin's prints.

"This is unheard of," he whispered to Kristin. "You're outselling all my old regulars. We're going to have to raise the prices on your next show."

Next show. Kristin dared not probe. She was afraid that if she examined any of the evening's highlights too carefully they would all vanish like a mirage under the weight of her scrutiny.

"There *will* be a next show, won't there?" It was Harrell Langston who pursued the possibility.

"Just say the word," Kristin gushed.

"Precisely the response I was hoping for." Harrell grinned. "Now that I've softened you up, why don't we step back into my office and make this all official by getting you to sign a contract to that effect? Wouldn't want some other gallery owner whisking away my discovery."

"Whose discovery?" Gray gibed, wrapping a possessive arm around Kristin's shoulders.

Kristin felt she could light up Diablo Peak with the internal incandescence she was generating. Woozy with champagne, she tilted her head back to lean against the hard shelf of Gray's chest. Her triumph felt complete.

"Before you two liquify into pools of contentment in front of my eyes," Harrell sighed, "could you please step into my office and sign a contract?"

Harrell's office was refreshingly quiet after the clamor of the reception. It smelled cozily of the pipe Harrell smoked occasionally. The walls were a patchwork of paintings, ceremonial masks, and intricate baskets. The desk was totally obscured beneath an avalanche of papers.

"Excuse the clutter," Harrell said offhandedly. "I wish I could say it isn't usually this messy in here, but I'm afraid this state is pretty standard. Clear off those chairs there. Just put those things anywhere."

Kristin obeyed, removing a stack of papers and files from the armchair opposite Harrell's desk. As she lowered the pile, a file folder flapped open, spilling its contents onto the floor.

"Here, let me get those." Harrell rushed to help Kristin.

"No, I've got it," she protested, scooping the assortment of papers back into the file. Gray bent beside her, his large hands dwarfing the papers he was helping her to gather up. As she was refilling the folder, a newspaper clipping on the top of the pile caught her eye. Kristin had only to read the first sentence—"A visit to the just-opened show at the Aperture Gallery, featuring the work of Kristin Jonsson, is like a visit to the candy store when one unwisely overindulges in the sugary confections"—to recognize Felicia Cliver's review of her first show.

"You knew." She looked up, glancing from Gray to Harrell. It was obvious that both had seen the devastating review. "You knew and you still let me go ahead with the show." Kristin was baffled.

"One look at your work," Harrell explained, "confirmed what I'd always suspected about Felicia Cliver. She wouldn't know good art if it came up and bit her on the leg. Seeing that pretentious old bag eat her words positively made my evening," he blurted out like a naughty schoolboy.

"I think there's really only one place to file this review," Gray said, plucking the scrap of newsprint from Kristin's fingers and holding it above the trash can. "And really only one appropriate way to proceed with the filing." He picked up a lighter from Harrell's desk and flicked it into flame beneath the clipping.

As Kristin watched the review turn to ashes that Gray

let drift into the trash can, she couldn't help feeling that the cloud that had been shadowing her life was finally gone, a shadow that had been cast by more than the burned review.

"Bravo!" Harrell applauded the burning in effigy.

Kristin looked at Gray. His darkly compelling features were obscured by a thin veil of smoke. Did he share her feeling? Had he too realized how easy it was to relegate bitter words and hurtful actions to the past, where they rightfully belonged?

"We should have done that a long time ago," Gray said.

"Yes, it was foolish of me to let that silly woman control my life," Kristin agreed, scrutinizing Gray for any hint of a reaction.

"Right," Gray chimed in forcefully, "let the past control history and let us control the present."

He feels the same way, Kristin silently exalted. He was ready at long last to leave behind the cruel remembrances his wife had left him. *Could this mean,* Kristin wondered desperately, *that he is ready to love again?*

"I'll drink to that," Harrell said, reaching into a desk drawer for a bottle of cognac and three snifters. All three raised their glasses and clinked them as Harrell proposed a toast "to the present."

But the wordless toast Kristin drank was to the future.

Chapter 11

D*o you have any plans* for this evening?" Gray asked, leaning toward Kristin after she'd signed the contract binding her to a one-woman show at the Langston Gallery.

"This evening has already exceeded my wildest imaginings; I couldn't possibly have planned it," Kristin answered. She'd overheard at least half a dozen people reminding Gray to stop by at various parties. He'd nodded and smiled noncommittally after each reminder. She imagined that he was going to ask her to join him on a round of party-hopping. She'd already decided to accept, but wished dispiritedly for a more intimate New Year's celebration.

"Would you like to join me at Le Piste Rouge for a late supper?" As if she needed convincing, Gray added, "Guillame has promised some exceptional delights tonight."

"I was afraid I was going to end up trailing around Taos following you up one slushy, luminaria-lighted sidewalk after another, trading pleasantries with strangers. An evening at a four-star French restaurant sounds heavenly in comparison."

They made their farewells to Eric, Betsy, Addie, and Harrell, who were all rushing off to an assortment of Taos parties, then climbed into Gray's Bronco for the trip up the mountain.

Powderhorn was a small village that looked as if it had been plucked straight out of the Swiss Alps. They drove through the snowy streets, passing shops with skis crossed in the darkened windows and tiers of hotel rooms ringing with the sounds of laughter and New Year's Eve merriment. Kristin had to keep reminding herself that, had it not been for Gray, Powderhorn Ski Valley would not exist. His energy, his vision had brought it all into being. Le Piste Rouge was tucked away off the main street. It was a grand two-story Victorian structure complete with a colonnaded front porch.

"This is one of the few houses that survived Powderhorn's first incarnation as a mining town," Gray explained, sliding into a parking place marked G. LOWREY, PROP.

"Mining? I didn't realize there had ever been any mining done up here."

"There wasn't a great deal. A bit of gold that proved not to be worth the time and effort to haul it out of the mountains. But while the boom was on, the mine owner had this house built for his wife, who was reputed to have been the most beautiful woman west of the Mississippi. Sort of the Taj Mahal of the Rockies."

"*Monsieur* Low-rey, *bonne année*," the maître d' snappily greeted Gray as they stepped inside, wishing him a happy New Year beneath a glittering chandelier and taking their coats.

"*Merci*, Alain."

"We have missed you, *monsieur.*"

"I've been rather busy."

"Will you have your usual room?" the dignified Frenchman inquired.

For a brief moment, indecision tangled Gray's expression. A second later it was gone and Gray spoke with his typical decisiveness. "Yes, Alain, we will."

Kristin was gawking so intently that she could barely keep pace as the maitre d' guided them through the magnificently renovated house. There was a main dining room where candles flickered at a dozen tiny tables, illuminating place settings of fine crystal and china in Le Piste Rouge's distinctive blue-rimmed pattern. A single rosebud graced each table. Shining silver wine buckets stood on tripods, waiting for attentive waiters who never let a glass go dry. Ornate, gilt-edged mirrors mounted throughout the room against wallpaper hand-printed with mountain columbines lent the room an airy Victorian splendor.

They passed into a chandelier-lighted corridor. Bustling waiters slid past, hurrying over the polished marble floor to cater to the needs of the smaller groups secluded in the rooms opening off of the hall.

"Et voilà, monsieur." Alain crisply swung open a door at the end of the polished hallway.

Inside was one impeccably set table. The rest of the room was comfortably furnished in refinished antiques. Alain swept aside a chair for Kristin.

"Tonight we have a *panache de poisson, coquille St. Jacques* . . ." The maître d' rattled off the house specialties in a welter of French with which Kristin could not even begin to keep up.

"Thank you, Alain; it all sounds exquisite, as usual. You may return for our order in a few minutes," Gray said, dismissing the Frenchman.

Kristin was grateful for Alain's departure; she hadn't wanted to display her ignorance in front of him.

"May I make a recommendation?" Gray asked.

"By all means."

"How about the *pâté* for an appetizer and the puff pastry stuffed with seafood for an entrée? And, of course, champagne."

"Mmm," Kristin murmured.

"I'll take that as approval."

When Alain had taken the order that Gray delivered in French and fetched a bottle of champagne, Gray again dismissed him, preferring to attend to the wine-opening ritual himself. Slowly, he eased the cork from the thick bottle, allowing only the slightest hint of the wine's natural effervescence to escape in a hazy cloud that drifted around the throat of the sea-green bottle.

"Magnifique," Kristin declared through the veil of bubbles in her throat.

"I didn't know you spoke French," Gray said, smiling. Like an animal who is never entirely at ease outside of its marked territory, he had been gripped by a slight tightness all evening. Here, master of his domain, he began to uncoil, the wariness vanishing. "I should have let you deal with Alain."

"Merci beaucoup, but you have just been treated to the entirety of my knowledge of the French language. And, while we're on the subject, how did a boy from the Kansas cornfields come to be so familiar with *panaches* and *pâtés?*"

"I was lucky; I had a very good teacher." Gray warmed visibly to the memory. "Jean-Luc. He was the sous-chef at Le Bistro de Pascal, a restaurant in Vail where I worked as a waiter in my ski-bum days. Anyway, Jean-Luc and I spent hours fantasizing about the 'real' French restaurant we would open one day. So, as soon as Powderhorn began turning a profit, I called him up and told him to start putting together the first four-star French restaurant in the Rockies. He concocted the menu and educated me about every item that went into it, then went to Paris to recruit a staff. He's there now trying to duplicate his success. He's going to open a second Piste Rouge for me down in the southern part of the state."

"You seem able to inspire a great deal of loyalty from those who work with you." The wine she had drunk put a sheltering haze between Kristin and her words, protecting her from their intimacy.

"I think that, in most cases, loyalty begets loyalty." His mouth, full and sensitive beneath the rougher barricade that was his beard, found the lip of the fluted crystal glass. To Kristin, watching Gray tilt the glass up until a rush of bubbles slammed against his lips, the moment was frozen in time, preserved in thick, amber candlelight. He lowered the glass, and Kristin forced herself to concentrate on the words formed by his moist lips.

"I am loyal," Gray stated flatly. "It's simply a characteristic I was born with, like having brown hair. When I commit myself, I do it without reservation; I hold nothing back."

Kristin no longer had to force herself to concentrate; she was hanging on Gray's words and listening even more intently to the meaning behind them, to what he was revealing about himself.

"Perhaps that's a mistake. In one case, it certainly was. But it's something I can't change."

His eyes, heavily lashed in sable brown, caught hers.

Firelight and anticipation danced in them. He tensed, leaning forward a bit in his chair. Kristin struggled to collect her wits, dragging them like rowdy drunkards out of the stuporous haze they'd stumbled into. She sensed that her response would carry a great deal of weight.

"Loyalty is a quality I appreciate," she said, meeting his searching gaze and holding it. "I sometimes think that I too err a bit on the side of dogged loyalty."

Gray relaxed and held his glass aloft. "To dogged loyalty."

Kristin joined Gray in his toast, feeling as if she'd passed a test she'd only dimly understood. There was a discreet rap at the door and a waiter entered, balancing a tray on his shoulder.

Kristin's *pâté* was served with crusty French bread. The teenager slid an artistically arranged plate with pinkish-red slices of salmon and white fish forming a sunburst pattern in front of Gray. "You've got to try this," Gray said after savoring the piquancy of the marinated fish.

Something about pressing forkfuls of food into each others' mouths in a four-star French restaurant just as they'd done at Raul's had them giggling like schoolchildren. They chuckled their way through bites of Kristin's crustaceans swimming in a buttery pastry shell full of a rich white sauce, swapped for tastes of Gray's veal served with a mushroom *forestière* sauce.

"I do believe," Gray announced, solemnly touching a napkin to his lips, "that on the International Bite Exchange, your scallops would take it over my veal."

"True, true," Kristin muttered gravely. "But your *panache* had it all over my *pâté.*"

Neither one could halt the eruption of giggles that possessed both of them when the haughty Alain appeared to inquire if "all was satisfactory."

"Not only satisfactory, but *magnifique,*" Kristin burst out, much to Gray's amusement.

Alain lost his monumental poise for only the barest fraction of a second as he saw his normally austere employer's face crinkling with suppressed laughter. He quickly collected himself and inquired whether they would be interested in dessert.

"I will send the waiter in with coffee then," he said, after the offered desserts had been declined.

"*Magnifique!*" Gray called after the Frenchman as he backed out the door, muttering in his native tongue. A chorus of champagne giggles followed him down the corridor. Gray looked ten years younger when he finally calmed himself. The dramatic change reminded Kristin of the incredible pressures he faced each day.

"You know," he mused, "I think that this is the first time I've ever really laughed in my own restaurant. I mean laughed like this until it hurt. There's been plenty of the kind of brittle laughter that goes with brittle, sophisticated witticisms, with the kind of evenings Jan was so fond of." His voice ground down to a raw edge. "But no real laughter, not until now. And we never did anything so gauche as eating off of each other's plates."

Gray's musings were interrupted by the appearance of a sterling-silver tray with a pot of coffee, cups, sugar, and cream on the table.

"Thank you, Etienne," Gray said, and the waiter left, gone for the evening.

The coffee was a rich French brew as pleasing to the palate as the rest of the extravagant meal had been.

"Gray," Kristin said, sighing as she leaned away from the table, "this has been the most opulent dining experience of my life."

"I'm glad. I wanted it to be just that. I was also glad to see you do the meal justice. It pains me when women pick at their food, wasting a magnificent meal for fear of either gaining a few ounces or letting the man they're with see that they have normal, healthy appetites."

"My appetite," Kristin confessed, "has always qualified as at least healthy and, on occasions like tonight, probably even robust."

"Yes," Gray concurred, "I've seen evidence of the robustness of your appetite."

Kristin colored, embarrassment heating her cheeks even more than the alcohol already had. There was no mistaking Gray's double entendre. It brought back the memory of his rebuffs with stingingly fresh humiliation. It also reminded Kristin of her vow never to let it happen again. She felt the gaiety of the evening fade away.

"Don't misinterpret me," Gray asked. "If there was one thing I admired about you from the start, it was your honesty, the way you could never hide what you felt or wanted."

"Why, then, have you always treated me as if I were harboring all sorts of dark and nasty motives? As if—" The wine unloosed the last knot holding Kristin's tongue in check. "As if I were your ex-wife all over."

Gray's nostrils flared and the jaw beneath his beard tightened. An icy film clouded his eyes. Then, in the time it takes to expel a pent-up breath, the mood of menacing fury vanished. "I deserved that." He spoke softly. "Shall I take you home now?" He scraped his chair back and rose to his full, intimidating height.

He towered over Kristin, looming above her like the cloud she thought she'd finally dispelled when Gray had burned the review earlier that evening. She felt poised on the edge of a precipice. She was being offered the choice of backing away from it, abandoning the unknown for the safe, the secure, or taking the plunge. She didn't know what lay beyond. She might plummet straight over the edge to be dashed on a shoal of treacherous rocks. Or she might float into a world as enchanted as this evening had been. It was she who would have to make the decision, take the risk. She and Gray could talk forever about loyalty, about trusting, about his ex-wife and she, inevitably, would end up running into the wall of his illogical fears. She had one chance of breaking through that barrier. With a dreamer's torpidity, she too rose to her feet. Gray was at her side, pulling back the delicately carved antique chair that the beautiful young wife of the mine owner had sat upon a century before.

Kristin's linen napkin fluttered to the floor. She ignored it and turned toward Gray. Like a stopwatch ticking away the seconds in a critical match, the grandfather clock at the end of the corridor pealed out the first of the twelve chimes of midnight. Wavering on the edge of the unknown, Kristin made her voice sound a boldness she didn't feel.

"I believe a good-luck kiss on the eve of a new year is customary."

"Kristin, you know what you're doing, don't you?" Gray spoke like a voice from a dream. The third chime rang, echoing down the hall.

"I don't care to discuss it," she answered, frosting her voice with a hint of imperiousness. The sound of it gave her courage. "Do you intend to honor the custom or not?" Three more chimes propelled them that much further into the future.

The room seemed to grow overheated, claustrophobic, as the seventh, then eighth chimes bonged out their message that a new year was about to begin. Kristin's false bravado abandoned her. She dropped her head and bent to retrieve the fallen napkin, the last of the chimes reverberating dully through her.

At the stroke of twelve, just when Kristin felt herself turning into an emotional pumpkin, two insistent hands descended, tucked themselves under her arms, and dragged her to her feet.

"It's too late," Gray whispered. Kristin looked into his face and saw what was on the dark edge of the precipice she had plunged over—a churning sea of passion. Gray's features were marked by a need so raw that Kristin was frightened by its intensity. Then the hands bracketing her breasts drew her closer and all Kristin's fears were washed away by the tidal wave of desire that swamped her, drowning her in the same sea that had engulfed Gray. They were the only creatures in that vast liquid universe. Kristin moved toward Gray.

His palms still touching the sides of her breasts, his fingers splayed across her back, he urged her closer. Kristin twined her arms around Gray's neck. His nearness, his smell, obliterated reason, vaporized logic. She kissed the tuft of hair that had so tantalized her earlier. The springy chest hairs against her lips made her think of lying down in a field of wildflowers and letting the grass and leaves and petals tickle her face with their sweetness.

Gray gathered her to him even more closely, cradling her head and tilting it up. He looked down and felt he had captured a creature from mythology—Diana, the goddess of the hunt, strong and fleet and more beautiful than even an immortal had a right to be. God, she felt good in his arms. She fit the way he'd always wanted a woman to fit without knowing it until now.

His hands found the openings at the kimono's armholes and slid in. Kristin gloried in the roughly stimulating feel of his questing hands against her bare skin. The sharp intake of her own breath whistled in her ears as the hands pivoted to cup the taut contours of her breasts, then began a gentle massage that sent a paralyzing languor sweeping through her. When his fingers found the hardened nubs at the center of those pliant mounds, his artful stimulation broke the stunned lethargy. Kristin arched toward him wanting more, wanting him. She pulled his head down.

The taste of her mouth on his was even sweeter for the delay. Gray savored it, a connoisseur who appreciated the pungency added by the excruciating weeks of denial.

For Kristin there was no reflection. Gray's kiss, at last whole and unrestrained, was a reality unto itself. His mouth seemed to suck up through her an aching wave of pleasure that lapped at her body with tongues of desire.

She stood on tiptoe, her breasts thrust even more fully into his hands by the action, and offered him more, of her lips, her body, her self.

The last thread of control was snapped. Gray's hands took on a frenzied life of their own, roaming wildly, seeking to know the body they held. His breathing was erratic, coming now in the same crazed rhythm that controlled Kristin's. He dragged his lips from hers, down the slanting curve of her jaw, to her earlobe, and on to the deliriously receptive column of her neck, the hollows at the base of her throat. The V of the kimono's neck lured him downward to the porcelain voluptuousness beyond. Her hardened nipples were plainly outlined beneath the thin fabric. First an enticement, the garment now became an intolerable barrier.

Gray noticed that his hands trembled as he reached out toward the sash he had knotted around her slender waist. He was sobered by a sense of monumental discovery, by the look of excruciating vulnerability in Kristin's eyes. For a moment he stayed the hand venturing forth and questioned for the millionth time the wisdom, the rightness, of what he was doing. All his lingering scruples, however, were incinerated in the dizzying heat that consumed him at the sight of the shadowy cleavage beneath the neckline of the silk kimono.

Kristin watched the stalled hands come back to life, felt them working against her stomach. The concho-laden sash fell with a muffled heaviness to the thickly carpeted floor. Gray parted the kimono, sliding it over Kristin's shoulders and letting it too slip to the floor.

"You're magnificent," he murmured, awed by the sight of Kristin's creamy white torso and high, proud breasts. He bent toward her, slipping one reverential hand beneath the full weight of her breast and lifting its dark-apricot center to his lips. The touch of his tongue against the maddeningly sensitized tips was unholy ecstasy. The wave of pleasure pulsed through Kristin again, leaving a spiraling vortex of desire whirling at her throbbing core.

Footsteps outside the door brought Kristin the clattering remembrance that they were in a restaurant. Gray straightened like a startled animal. Kristin crossed her hands in front of her breasts.

"Come," Gray ordered her, holding out his hand.

When Kristin didn't move, too drugged by passion and too fearful of exposure to act, Gray scooped her into his arms as easily as he whisked little Laurie off her feet. In a remote corner of her mind, Kristin registered the fact that this was a first. No other man she'd ever known had done what Gray had accomplished so effortlessly. He carried her toward a door that she had assumed led to a long-defunct closet.

"Open it." His voice was husky and freighted with the urgent burden of desire. Kristin leaned an arm down and twisted the knob, opening a door onto a staircase. They ascended. At the top was another door that opened into a large bedroom.

"We had the main staircase taken out when we converted the house into a restaurant," Gray explained, settling her onto the king-sized bed covered with an antique quilt.

"I don't want to hear about it," Kristin hushed him. She had no interest in the *we* of Gray's past. She didn't want to know about the bed she lay in or the room that sheltered her. The only *we* she had any interest in at that moment was the *we* she and Gray formed.

"You're wise." He turned to touch a match to the fire already laid in the room's hearth. It burst into flame instantly, chasing the chill and mustiness from the room. His back lighted by the flames, Gray turned to Kristin. Her hair, a copper fan spread out over the pillow, caught the color of the fire and reflected it back with an added brilliance. Unruly tendrils tumbled around her face in a cascade of curls, trickling over her shoulders and twining about her breasts. The gilded firelight glanced off her moist lips, her luminous skin, the feral wildness lurking in the depths of those unearthly green eyes. It was all Gray could do to hold himself in check, to keep himself from going to her to feast on her loveliness. He crossed his arms and slipped off his sweater, then bent an arm over his chest and unbuttoned the sleeve of his shirt with a restraining slowness that was at excruciating odds with the primitive impulses beating through his blood. Two instincts warred within him. He wanted Kristin with a fearsome urgency. But he also wanted to make this moment last as long as it possibly could. Once his shirt was removed, he unbuckled his belt and his pants. The weight of the conchos remaining on the belt stripped his pants away. His eyes held Kristin's as he removed the final barrier.

He's exquisite, Kristin thought, so struck by Gray's physical perfection that she felt momentarily detached from it. He looked as if he'd stepped out of a myth, fresh from riding a winged horse or slaying a one-eyed giant. Kristin had never even dreamed of a man like Gray. The size of him, the aura of controlled strength, his masculine sureness, all combined to make her feel fragile and feminine. The experience was excitingly novel. He moved toward her. Seeing his superbly conditioned body in motion was like watching the sculptures of Greek athletes she had studied in art class come to life. He stopped at the foot of the bed and, with Kristin's collaboration, tugged the harem pants free of her ankles.

His gaze on her nude form warmed Kristin far more effectively than the fire did. It traced a smoldering trail from her eyes, down the delicate ridges of her rib cage, across the flattened drum that was her stomach, to the puff of coppery hair at the juncture of her impossibly long, pale legs.

"You're too beautiful to be real," he murmured, echoing her exact thoughts about him.

She unfolded her arms, aching now for the sweet pressure of his glorious body. His heat seared her length as he laid his body on top of hers. He cupped his hands about her heart-shaped buttocks and pulled her to him, pressing her against himself with a devastating contact that told of the extravagant extent of his desire.

"God, woman, I've wanted you." His words were a hoarse, insensate rumbling against her ear. Her response was a kiss that spoke even more eloquently of her longing, a longing that had been denied far too long.

"Please, Gray." Her plea issued from a spot deep within her that Kristin had never known existed. She was burningly ready for his desire. When Gray settled his weight upon her, it was like the fulfillment of a promise. They moved together as one, guided only by thoughts of the other's pleasure, pleasure that rapidly became their own. This recycling of sensation amplified it to a height Kristin had never before scaled. Higher and higher she was dragged until she felt herself hurtling into a black void that was the culmination of all sensation.

Kristin returned to earth to find herself cradled in the security of Gray's arms. As the fury of their lovemaking subsided, he stroked back the damp tendrils of hair clinging to her forehead and feathered kisses on the dewy skin beneath.

"Mmm." Deep in her throat Kristin made a growl of utter animal contentment as she rolled into his grasp, burying her face in the musky male smell of his chest.

"You have hair, wonderful, springy hair. A pampa of hair all over your chest," she rhapsodized, more intoxicated by love than champagne.

Gray held her away so that he could see her face. "What, were you afraid I'd be some hairless eunuch?" His laugh was as rich and warm and cozy as a cup of good coffee on a cold morning.

"I really didn't have much firsthand evidence before, did I?" Kristin teased. "You were so busy fighting me off that I never really got a chance to find out." She propped herself up on an elbow and Gray rolled onto his back. "Are you sorry now that you finally succumbed?" she asked playfully, although a sudden sharp stab of panic alerted her that she still feared his response, his power to crush her with yet another rejection.

A grin that started at his toenails lighted Gray's face. "Hardly. I've wanted you so badly for these past months, ever since Diablo Peak—hell, ever since you walked into my office—that I've been in agony. I'd lie awake at night imagining what you looked like underneath all those damned woolens. Wondering if you could possibly be as wondrously creamy as you are." His hands slid over the dip of her waist, the swell of her hips, and rested with a comforting possessiveness on her rounded bottom. Everywhere they brushed they created a tingling reawakening.

"'Wondrously creamy.'" Kristin repeated his description. "I *do* like that."

"What about me?" he asked, a taunting gleam in his eye. "No lyricism for this battered old bod?"

"How about wondrously steamy?" Kristin suggested with a mock sultriness, running her hand over his sweat-dampened forehead. "Or wondrously dreamy?" The playful sultriness was replaced by a more genuine emotion as Kristin trailed her hand over the swells of Gray's luxuriously muscled shoulders and chest. Her fingers lingered on the bony promontory that jutted up, marking his pelvis. It was shiny with old scar tissue.

"What happened here?" Her voice sounded rusty and slow, like someone talking in her sleep.

She felt more than heard the bass rumble of a slight chuckle. "Acute skinniness. I couldn't eat enough to keep up with my growth when I was younger, and those bones stuck out even more than they do now. So far, in fact, that my pants rubbed the skin over them raw." He laughed slow and easy. "They used to call me Hanger because, for a while, that's how my clothes fit me—just dropping straight off my shoulders."

"Poor Hanger," Kristin purred as she slithered down to plant a kiss on the old wound.

"'Poor Hanger,' indeed," Gray gibed, catching Kristin

and pulling her back up to him. "You shouldn't have done that; the old Hanger's not as wiry as he used to be." The light, bantering tone left his voice. Gray was solemn now in a way that alerted Kristin to listen closely. "I'm not made of metal," he finished, searching her face for a sign that she had understood what he was really telling her.

"No, Gray," she answered, his solemnness now hers as well. "Neither am I."

He hugged her to him in a fierce embrace. Then, with her thighs straddling the old scars, they began to love one another again.

Chapter 12

The moon was full on that first night of the new year. It streamed into the bedroom in broad ribbons of platinum. Kristin was glad for the light. Although her body was exhausted, her mind whirled, speeding to digest all the day's events, then stopping breathlessly at the recollection of what had capped them. She edged herself up into a sitting position, careful not to wake Gray, who had fallen into a fitful sleep with his arms still tangled around her.

The light from a high bay window nearby puddled around their bed, submerging it in a shimmering pool. Kristin stole the opportunity to study the man who had dominated her thoughts for so many weeks. Seeing him now, it was hard to believe he could have caused her such misery. Asleep, the covers tugged down around his waist, Gray looked like a little boy in a Halloween beard. His skin had the luminous radiance usually possessed only by young children; his dark eyelashes were a smoky shadow against his tanned cheeks. At his throat a vein throbbed with a steady, unwavering beat. Kristin brought a hand up to settle, light as a snowflake, upon that indefatigable pulse. She felt life pump through Gray. It seemed almost as if some of that force spilled over at the feather-soft contact and coursed up through Kristin's trembling fingertips to flood her with a drowning excess of emotion. She could no longer contain it within herself.

"I love you," she whispered, barely giving the words voice. "I love you," she said again, this time to herself, to let the inescapable truth sink in.

Gray stirred; his features, in such placid repose a moment before, stiffened against the nightmare playing out on the screen of his mind. Kristin pulled her hand away, letting it hover above him as she wondered whether to wake him. But his features unclenched, he sighed, and then he rolled away from Kristin. She settled the covers back up around them and snuggled up next to Gray, molding her body to the shield of his back, and slept.

Warm, buttery sunshine nudged Kristin awake. Gray was already up. Kristin watched drowsily as he positioned a tray holding a pot of coffee and a plate of rolls on top of a chest of drawers.

"You're awake," Gray observed.

"Not really," Kristin replied sleepily. "My eyes are open; that's all. My mind is still in a coma."

"You can sleep the whole day away if you'd like. I've already sent an instructor over to High Country to cover your lessons."

A jolt of alarm shot through Kristin. She'd completely forgotten her responsibilities.

"Don't worry." Gray smiled, seeing Kristin's distress. "I doubt that your career as a cross-country ski instructor is destined to last much longer anyway, now that you've signed on for a one-woman show at Harrell's gallery."

"It really did happen? I didn't just dream the whole evening?"

The bed lowered as Gray sat down beside her. "It happened," he said, brushing a kiss across her forehead. "Every bit of it happened." The memory of the previous night's passion flared between them. Breaking the contact, Gray stood and went to fetch the tray he'd brought in. "Now, how about some breakfast?"

Kristin sat up, clutching the bedcovers to her. The dry pounding in her skull reminded her of the evening's overindulgence. "Maybe just a cup of coffee. Black," she specified as Gray poured.

"Sure I can't tempt you with one of Guillame's croissants? You won't find any better this side of the Seine," Gray promised.

Kristin shook her aching head no. But, by the time she'd finished the cup of coffee, her appetite had returned and she took the crescent-shaped roll.

"You'll need your energy," Gray observed.

"Why?"

"Why? To ski Powderhorn, of course."

"Gray, I ski cross-country, not downhill. Or had you forgotten?"

"You may not know it," Gray corrected her, "but you ski downhill. I saw you come down Diablo Peak, and you came as close to downhill as a person can on cross-country skis. So, let's get rolling—I want to show you my mountain."

Kristin scampered off to the bathroom, buoyed up by a sense of discovery and adventure. Anything that she and Gray did together this day would be perfect.

"There are ski clothes in the closet," Gray called through the bathroom door. "I'm going to see about equipment for you."

"Gray." Kristin stopped his departure after her first glimpse of the bathroom. "I never realized what a hedonist you are." She poked her head around the door. "This bathroom looks like something out of ancient Rome."

Gray shrugged uncomfortably at the reference to the opulent room furnished with mirrored tiles on the walls, a sunken bathtub, a Jacuzzi, and more oils, creams, and perfumes than Kristin had ever seen outside of a drugstore. "It wasn't my idea." The way he said it told Kristin more clearly than words that the idea had been Jan's. She regretted immediately having brought up the subject.

"I'll be right back." Gray left quickly.

Kristin ignored the decadent splendor of the marbled tub and took a brisk shower. From a cedar-lined cabinet, she extricated the only towel that wasn't plush velour and monogrammed with the initials JL and vigorously rubbed herself dry.

The clothes she found in the closet weren't monogrammed, but they were marked just as clearly by a stylish elegance that told Kristin who had chosen them: Jan. Just as she had chosen all the exquisitely tasteful antiques that sat about the bedroom Gray and his ex-wife had once shared. The furniture, the clothes—everywhere she turned Kristin found new evidence of Jan's all-pervasive touch.

Kristin weeded through the selection of stretch jumpsuits and outlandishly colored parkas and sweaters, debating whether she could bear to put on any of the garments. For a few minutes, she wavered, seriously considering wrapping herself up in Gray's parka and retreating to High Country. No, she stopped herself, that would be tantamount to surrendering one more bit of Gray's life to Jan's control, and the woman already had more than her share. Kristin stomped back to the closet and found a subdued outfit of navy-blue stretch pants and a pale-blue sweater.

"Nice choice," Gray commended her as he stepped back into the room. "If I weren't so set on showing you Powderhorn, I'd seriously consider making a detailed comparison of the question at hand."

"What question?" Kristin asked, pleased that Gray had shaken off the dark mood that had threatened earlier.

"Why, the question of whether you are more tempting *in* clothes or out of them."

"Come on," Kristin laughed, "let's have a look at this mountain of yours."

"You're right; there will be time later on—all the time we need."

Kristin tried to keep herself from putting too much store in what might have been a casual statement, but she didn't succeed. She believed it was impossible that Gray could have been unmoved by their night together. That the love she felt could be anything but mutual. She followed Gray downstairs.

The restaurant, never open for breakfast, was deserted. Only a dim, muffled clatter came from the kitchen, where the chef's assistants were beginning to simmer the stock and herbs that would form the base of the evening's sauces. The smell of the croissants that had been baked earlier that morning hung in the air, overpowering the odor of last night's dinners. A trail of forgotten confetti led down the hall.

Outside, the new year had dawned crisp and cold. Skiers, skis crossed over their shoulders, bustled down the main street, walking like gawky spacemen in their molded-plastic ski boots and bulky down-filled outfits. A contingent of outlaw skiers—the males in swooping cowboy hats, the women with bandannas around their necks—passed by in a cloud of raucous chatter. A couple, she in canary yellow, he in tomato red, their two children in hot pink and orange, next caught her eye. Purist though she was, Kristin had to admit that on this particular morning, with Gray by her side, the downhill-ski fashion spectacle with its riot of crayon colors delighted her, reflecting as it did the joy-colored rainbow of her emotional state.

For his part, Gray looked every inch the master of all he surveyed. In his ski boots he stood six and a half feet tall. He wore a black-and-red sweater with a Scandinavian design around the yoke and a pair of charcoal-gray ski pants. Atop his head sat a hat of Russian wolf.

"Well, you haven't told me what you think of it yet." Gray came to a dead stop in the midst of the hustling crowd and swept an arm up toward "his" mountain.

"I've been so busy gawking that I really haven't—" Kristin's train of words was derailed by her first real look at Powderhorn Mountain. The great mountain loomed over the Alpinesque village like a giant who'd risen up behind them as big and silent as the moon. Kristin only dimly heard Gray's exposition of the facilities.

"We've got over sixty trails served by half a dozen double chair lifts and I don't know how many cable lifts. Timberline is at twelve thousand feet here. That's twice as high as it is in the Alps."

"My God, it's intimidating," Kristin breathed. The giant of a mountain looked like it had on a white bib with dark dribbles of trails running down at dangerously steep angles.

"Yours is such a common reaction to Powderhorn," Gray calmed her, "that I had this little sign put up."

Kristin hauled her eyes from the mountain to the sign Gray indicated. It read, DON'T PANIC! YOU ARE LOOKING AT ONLY A SMALL FRACTION OF POWDERHORN'S TOTAL SKI AREA. POWDERHORN OFFERS MANY LESS-CHALLENGING TRAILS. ENJOY SKIING AT YOUR OWN LEVEL.

"Good advice," Kristin muttered. "I only hope that there are trails here easy enough for my level."

"Oh, there are," Gray promised. "You're looking at Suicide Alley and Gray's Folly now, the two hardest runs on the mountain."

"Gray's Folly?" Kristin inquired.

"It's my favorite trail," Gray explained. "Originally, I named it Joe's Run after a Native American fellow who works for the Forest Service that I used to ski with. But,

on the day I introduced him to that trail, Joe started calling it Gray's Folly. He claimed that I'd created a trail too steep to ski. Anyway, that name caught on better than Joe's Run, so Gray's Folly it is."

Gray described the run with warm familiarity, as if he were discussing an old friend that he and Kristin had in common.

"That run, as intimidating as it is, was what kept Powderhorn in business when I was just getting started. Skiers from all over the country would hear about the trail too steep to be skied and come to Powderhorn to take it on. Just like upstart gunslingers in the Old West taking on whomever the legend of the time was. I wish you could have seen it then."

Kristin saw the glimmer in Gray's eyes that the memory of those early days evoked. "I wish I could have too."

"Well, the trail's still here, still tough as it ever was. Want to give it a try?"

"Thanks, no, not on my first day," Kristin replied dryly.

"I was joking. I would never have allowed you on something that steep."

Kristin felt oddly comforted by his burst of protectiveness.

"No, we'll start off on Bambino this morning, then move on to Powder Puff."

"Now those are names I can live with," Kristin agreed.

"None of these Follies and Suicides for me, thank you very much."

"Come on," Gray said, swinging an arm around Kristin's shoulder, "let's get some of that white stuff under our skis."

Kristin's first ride up the cable lift to the top of the bunny hill was a howling disaster. She ended up toppling into a snowbank and pulling Gray in with her when he attempted to help her up. On her next ride, Gray had her perch atop the seat he formed with his thighs and, his arms around her waist, they made it to the top. Kristin had so many years of experience in balancing on two narrow slats of wood already trained into her nerves and muscles that this new variation came fairly rapidly. In no time she had conquered the beginners' slope.

"That was fast," Gray declared as she swooshed to a stop beside him. "You're ready to take a trip to the top of the hill."

"As long as the return route doesn't involve Suicide Alley or your Folly."

"Guaranteed."

The chair lift afforded Kristin a rare vantage point. As the chair, strung from a cable overhead, shuttled them up the mountain, Kristin felt as if she were sailing through the cornflower-blue sky. She squirmed around to see the sweep of the valley as it rolled away toward Taos. Ahead, a plume of spindrift whirled off the snowy mountainside, shattering the sunlight into a dry rainbow that danced past Kristin and Gray.

"Your mountain is quite nice," she said in deliberate understatement.

"Glad you approve."

At the top of the mountain, Gray guided her down the chute that led skiers away from the chair lift's terminus toward the trails that spoked away from it in every direction. The dry powder squeaked beneath Kristin's skis while a relentless wind churned over the titanic hunk of granite. The ceaseless current had carved the snow into exquisite sculptures called cornices. They curled over the summit like a line of waves caught forever at the moment just before breaking onto a frozen beach.

All was calm farther on, where the mountain sheltered them. Gray went ahead, deliberately exaggerating his motions to provide a model for Kristin to follow. With a little practice, she found the rhythm he was setting. She swayed with it, jutting out a hip and pricking a pole tip into the snow to initiate a turn, then swinging her weight around to shift it to the other ski and complete the turn. Down the mountain from her, Gray skidded to a snow-spraying halt to observe. Suddenly Kristin became acutely aware of her form.

"Bend *zee* knees. Keep *zee* weight forward," Gray called out, jokingly giving a French version of the ski instructor's most common bits of advice.

"If nothing else," she panted, trying to catch her breath as she slid to a stop beside Gray, "this experience has given me a new empathy for my students. It's really hard doing *anything* when you know you're being scrutinized. Especially by someone you—" The word *love* almost bubbled out of her spontaneously, but Kristin caught herself in time. "Someone you're trying to impress," she amended.

"Well, you're doing spectacularly well. I knew you'd take to downhill, but you've surprised even me." Gray craned his neck, looking off into the stand of pines that lined the trail. "I wonder where they put those wineskins. There's usually one somewhere right around here."

"Wineskins? What are you muttering about?"

"Ah-ha," Gray declared victoriously, swinging his skis around, "just as I thought. There's one hanging from that spruce right over there." He jetted off the trail with one forceful thrust of his poles. Slightly bewildered, Kristin followed the grooves his skis dug into the deep, unpacked powder. At their end, Gray was unhooking the strap of a leather wineskin from a pine-needled bough.

"We set out a dozen or so of these every morning," Gray explained, untwisting the cap, "to refresh the weary skier who happens to stumble upon their hiding places." He tilted his head back and directed a burgundy stream into his mouth. "Lean your head back," he directed, aiming the wineskin her way.

"I think I'll pass," Kristin demurred. "After last night, abstinence might be the best course for me to steer for a while."

"Just a sip," Gray urged. "It's part of the Powderhorn tradition. Then we'll cap it up for the next wayfaring skier. Come on, open up."

"All right, but just a sip," she cautioned, throwing her head back too. Gray scooted closer to her, straddling her skis with his, and directed an unerring trickle through her open lips. The wine tingled in her mouth with a fruity richness. A few purple drops dribbled onto her chin as Gray halted the flow. Kristin was pulling off her leather glove to wipe them away when Gray intervened.

"Allow me," he requested with a mock courtliness, bending toward her and licking the errant drops of wine from her chin.

"Is that part of the Powderhorn tradition too?" Kristin asked.

"No, and neither is this." His lips were warm, his kiss winy. He let the wineskin fall to the snow, where a few crimson drops stained the whiteness, and pulled her to him. Kristin slid forward. The track her skis were on led her to a dangerously provocative position between Gray's legs. Although thick layers of clothing separated them, Kristin felt the arousal that flared through Gray.

"God, woman," he said, breathing rapidly, "what you do to me is positively criminal. Damn all these clothes. I feel like we're two Eskimos meeting on some ice floe. We should be rubbing noses."

"Hugging is quite nice too," Kristin said, snuggling as close as her bulky parka and his sweater would allow.

"True," Gray agreed huskily. "As a matter of fact, hugging you is a lot more than nice. Have you noticed how we fit together like two pieces of a matched set?"

"Mmm," Kristin purred. "Matched tallness. More than nice."

"Have you noticed how we seem to belong together?"

Gray's tone alerted Kristin that he was talking about far more than the way their bodies conformed. "Yes, Gray," she answered with deliberate care, "I've noticed. I was wondering if you had." Her breath caught in her chest, unwilling to come out until she'd heard what Gray's answer would be.

"I've noticed, Kristin—more than you're aware of. Believe me, I've noticed." Their thoughts seemed to flow together, crystallizing in the frosty vapor that escaped as they breathed to mingle in a common cloud above their heads. For a moment, Gray appeared to be on the verge of giving voice to the unspoken thoughts hovering about them as thick as the steam they exhaled. Instead, he touched Kristin's bottom lip and asked, "Are you cold or is your lip stained blue from the wine?"

"I'm not warm," Kristin confessed, though she would

have gladly stood up to her knees in ice to hear what she dared not hope Gray had been about to say.

"Shall we continue this conversation down at the lodge in front of the fire?"

"I'll vote for that."

"All right," Gray grinned, "duck down." As she squatted down, he slid easily over her. "Now, I'll race you down."

"Gray, you'll beat—"

Kristin's protest was interrupted. "I'll give you a fifteen-minute head start."

Kristin made a rapid calculation: With any luck she could reach the bottom in that amount of time. "You're on," she called out, poling away briskly. Back on the trail, Kristin concentrated on maintaining a steady, even pace. If she didn't take any major tumbles, she just might make it. The heavier skis with their metal edges bit into the snow more forcefully than the lighter, cross-country ones she was used to. But, by visualizing how Gray had looked carving sweeping linked turns into the mountain ahead of her, Kristin made the unruly skis behave. She kept her knees well bent so that they could act as shock absorbers, soaking up jolts from any unexpected bumps or moguls. Soon the skis lost their strangeness and she fell into a rolling rhythm, dancing from one to the other.

Finally, the trail opened up and Kristin could see

the base of the chair lift and the lodge far below. She allowed herself to stop long enough to catch her breath and glance back over her shoulder. There was no sign of Gray. She wondered if her fifteen-minute head start had expired and if Gray was already bearing down on her. She tucked a few wisps of hair back under her woolly cap, zipped her parka up to the bottom of her chin, and pushed off again. If nothing else, she wanted to make a good showing in front of Gray.

Gray. The name competed with the mountain for her attention. Though she focused on the trail ahead, the memory of the night before captured her physical attention, leaving her body feeling more wobbly than skiing over a chunky series of moguls did. Luckily, she was nearly to the bottom. Odd, she thought, that Gray hadn't whizzed past her yet. She set her edges against the snow near the chair lift. It was packed hard from the ceaseless compacting of hundreds of skis, and she skidded a good way across the icy surface before coming to a stop.

She turned, expecting to see Gray seconds behind her. After a brief moment of self-congratulation in which Gray still did not appear, she became slightly worried. Then she heard the lift operator call to his helper, "Hey, look, Gray's taking on the Folly."

Kristin's gaze snapped back to the top of the mountain, where she instantly picked out a red-and-black blur winding down the treacherous slope. From that distance, he appeared almost to be floating down the impossible trail. But Kristin knew that was an illusion. In her mind, she heard the scrape of Gray's metal ski edges against the trail slanted so steeply that loose snow tumbled off of it, leaving only ice to cling to its granite contours. Only the relaxed jesting of the lift operators caused her heart to unfreeze.

"He's still got it, doesn't he?"

"Got it? He *owns* that run. No one can ski the Folly like Gray."

The chair lift creaked to a halt as the two operators abandoned it to devote their full attention to Gray's descent. All the skiers trapped on the motionless chairs joined in watching this unknown skier in the red-and-black sweater hurtle down a trail few of them would ever attempt.

As Kristin watched, a skier near the end of the trail fell. Because Gray's Folly was so steep and so slick, the hapless skier continued sliding until he came to the flat runoff at the trail's end.

"Lucky he didn't fall higher up," the lift operator commented.

"Yeah," his helper agreed. "I've seen 'em tumble at about where Gray is now, and since there's nothing up there to stop the slide, they shoot down the mountain like a rocket. Hit a tree or something and it's all over."

Don't let him fall, God, Kristin whispered under her

breath. The realization of how truly fragile he was, how easily he could be plucked away from her, suffused Kristin with the full knowledge of how immeasurably precious he was to her. In spite of the anxiety pounding through her, she was able to marvel at the reflexes, control, and strength that could make Gray's performance possible. After a few more agonizing minutes, Gray reached the runoff. He crouched into a racing stance and flew over the remaining yards. Kristin's boots were sprinkled by the ice Gray's skis scraped loose as he braked to a stop.

"Way to go, man," the lift operator called out to his boss as he engaged the gears that started the chair lift in motion again.

"Thanks, Carl," Gray answered between gulps of air that expanded his chest beneath the patterned sweater. He leaned forward on his poles like a marathoner catching his breath at the end of the course. When he straightened back up, he caught Kristin's eye and came toward her.

"You won." He smiled.

"I didn't come down Gray's Folly," she reminded him.

"That was for you," he whispered. "I wanted to give you one perfect red rose this morning, but none was available. So I had to settle for one perfect run. Or as close to perfect as I could come."

"Any more perfect," Kristin answered, "and I would have needed CPR."

Gray was just about to make a comeback when a young woman came out of the lodge calling his name.

"What is it, Denise?" Gray asked, once again the man in charge.

"There's a call for you waiting in your office. From California."

Gray's face, a ruddy palette of tanned exertion a moment before, whitened. Using the tip of his pole, he popped the release mechanism on his skis, stepped out of them, shrugged off his poles, and abandoned both as he strode off toward the lodge as rapidly as the heavy boots would allow. Kristin removed her equipment and gathered it and Gray's up. She propped them on the rack outside the lodge.

Inside, the main hall of Powderhorn's lodge was as sleek and elegant as High Country's was homey. Chicly dressed skiers were clustered around tables drinking, flashing inhumanly white smiles at one another, and making the kind of perky, brittle conversation that always made Kristin feel uncomfortable. She asked a man selling slices of quiche behind a counter where the office was. He directed her toward a long hall that twisted around to the back of the lodge.

Kristin tapped at a closed door marked simply POWDERHORN OFFICE. There was no response, but she could hear the rumble of Gray's voice. She opened the door a crack, intending to catch Gray's eye, wave to let him know she was waiting, then step back outside. But Gray was standing with his back to her when she opened the door, his every word clear.

"Don't cry, baby." He was soothing, his voice in that special register he reserved for speaking to Laurie. "I know you're lonely and I'm glad you called. That was very smart of you to find the piece of paper with Daddy's phone number on it. No, of course you don't have to stay there anymore. Tell Jan—" He broke off before his tone, which was gaining in force, got any louder. Then he started again. "Tell Mommy to call me as soon as she comes home. Okay, darling?"

He was silent as his daughter spoke words Kristin could only guess at.

"I love you too, Button. Don't worry about anything anymore. Daddy will take care of everything. You'll be home before you know it. Bye-bye, Button." Gray stood for a moment, the phone still cradled at his ear, before he turned with a savage swiftness and slammed down the receiver. "That bitch," he hissed. His hand trembling with impotent rage, he looked up to find Kristin staring at him. "Laurie is all alone out there," he said with a kind of helpless misery, slumping into the chair behind the desk.

Kristin came to his side. "What do you mean?"

"I mean, Jan has left her with no one to look after her, and this isn't the first time. God, what possessed me to think that a woman with the instincts of an alley cat could ever change? Laurie is a special child who needs special care. I knew that. I've learned that few people are capable of caring enough. Probably no one could who hasn't known her since she was a baby. Hasn't loved her since then." His words trailed off as the clutch of worry and fear wrapped around him.

The sound of glasses rattling and a high, shrill laugh drifted in from the main hall. Suddenly those happy sounds seemed terribly far off. She watched Gray as his strong hands twined around one another and she said the only thing she could.

"She'll be all right, Gray. I'm sure she will."

He nodded, and they sat together in a silence filled with unvoiced worry. The ring of the phone was like an alarm going off. Gray ripped the receiver out of its cradle.

"Jan?" he demanded. The pause that followed was brief. "Where the hell have you been? You're damned right I'm mad. No, Laurie is *not* old enough to be left alone. Laurie may never be old enough to be left alone. But you never could face that fact, could you?"

He drew in a quivering inhalation and began again. "Look, Jan, I'm sorry. It won't help Laurie for us to argue. Just take her to the airport and put her on the first plane back to New Mexico. Yes, I'm sure she wants to come home. Yes, Jan, just do it, please. For once, do what's best for Laurie. Of course I'll let her come to visit again. Bye,

Jan." As he put the phone down, he murmured to himself, "She'll never see Laurie again as long as I'm alive."

After he'd phoned every airline with flights from Los Angeles to Albuquerque and determined which flight his daughter would most likely be coming in on, Gray finally fully acknowledged Kristin's presence.

"I'm going to have to drive down to Albuquerque. If Jan gets her over to the airport in time, Laurie can make a flight that leaves in a few hours. I doubt that she will, but I'd better go now anyway."

"Would you like me to come with you?" Kristin asked.

"No, I'd better go alone. Laurie is likely to be fairly upset. As a matter of fact," he went on, glancing away, "it might be better all around if you weren't here at all when we returned."

"Weren't here?" she asked. Although Kristin had planned on going back to High Country, she was stunned by Gray's point-blank order to do so.

Gray's hands clenched and unclenched as if he were forcing himself to unloose his grip on something he wanted very much to hang on to. "Yes. I don't think it would be good for Laurie to see us together. To know that there was anything between us."

"Is there anything between us?" she inquired in a low voice.

"It might be better"—Gray's words came out slowly, with long pauses between each one—"if there weren't."

Kristin felt as if a pit had just opened up at a point below her sternum. An icy pit of fathomless depth. With eyes that no longer felt connected to her brain, she watched Gray change out of his ski boots and slip on some shoes in preparation for the drive to Albuquerque.

"So that's it," she muttered, barely able to form the words. "Just like that. 'It might be better if there weren't anything between us' and you're gone."

"Kristin, this isn't easy for me."

"Why not?" she snapped. "You've had enough practice. Twice already with me, and who knows how many times with other women? Are you going to tell me now that we should be friends? Like your 'friend' at the dress shop? Is that it? Am I supposed to be a friend like that?"

"Kristin, you don't understand. What I feel for you is—" Gray shook his head as if he could dislodge the feeling he'd come perilously close to divulging. "Forget it, it doesn't matter. What I feel is of no importance anymore. It never was. Hasn't been since Laurie was born. I almost forgot that."

In a moment of decision, Kristin made an instantaneous and irrevocable vow that she would not become like the shop owner, would not let the anger she felt dissolve into a sickly morass of lonely depression that would keep her trapped within a pit of unrequited love. "Don't tell me about Laurie," she blazed. "Don't use her as your shield against commitment or whatever it is you're frightened of. Nothing about me or anything we could have had together, Gray Lowrey, would have ever harmed that child."

"I can't risk it, Kristin. I can't take the chance of Laurie's becoming attached again. She's not an ordinary child."

"No child is ordinary. And no relationship comes with a guarantee. You risk what you want to risk in life. So don't use Laurie as an excuse for your cowardice."

"I'm doing what I think is best for my child." Gray's eyes pleaded for her understanding. Kristin turned from them; she had listened to their plea once too often.

"I'll be leaving High Country," she stated with a flat finality. "I'll stay only long enough for you to find a replacement and"—here she paused to make sure that Gray understood her seriousness, because she had already made up her mind about the next point—"to say goodbye to Laurie. In spite of all you've done to keep her from the dreaded fate of becoming attached to another human being, I think she is fond of me. I know I am of her. I don't want to simply disappear from her life the way Jan did, the way you apparently want me to. It wouldn't be fair to her. If you'd like, I can come here. You can arrange to be elsewhere. Actually, I'd prefer it if you were."

"No," Gray mumbled, shattered by Kristin's unexpected vehemence, "I'll bring her by before she goes back to Santa Fe."

"Good," she said, standing brusquely. "Could you have someone take me back to High Country? I'll be waiting out in the main hall."

Gray nodded numbly. For a brief moment, seeing the grief crumbling his face, Kristin felt the hot core of her own grief-fueled anger cool. She pivoted sharply to escape the weakening, to flee before the artificial starch stiffening her words and backbone dissolved. Then, her hand trembling with rage and pain, Kristin closed the door on Gray Lowrey.

Chapter 13

The *new year grew old* very quickly for Kristin. The day after she returned from Powderhorn, Addie delivered a message from Gray saying that a replacement instructor would arrive in a week and asking if she could please stay that long.

"Don't tell me you're leaving us," Addie wailed. But Kristin's tight-jawed nod prevented the lodge manager from making any further protest.

Even Punkin' sensed the extent of Kristin's sadness. The affable dog no longer gamboled about the room in the morning, eager for Kristin to dress and take her downstairs. She waited patiently as her mistress slumped out of bed, weary from a night filled with more tears than sleep. Punkin' sniffed at her for signs and smells of ill health, clues to her lethargy, and sensed something even more distressing than sickness.

Hearing the nightly sobs, Punkin' heaved herself to her feet and, nails clicking against the hardwood floor, went to investigate. The retriever dropped her big, chunky head on the bed, her sorrowful eyes reflecting what they saw—Kristin locked in a fetal curl of misery, tears slipping from her eyes to a wet darkened spot on the pillow. Kristin didn't even roll over to reach out a hand to pat her visitor, something she had never failed to do in the past. A sigh flapped out the sides of the dog's black mouth and she plodded back to her rug.

Eric and Betsy too felt powerless in the face of Kristin's emotional devastation. They saw her as she attempted to teach classes, her voice setting out strong then trailing off like a record on a stereo when the plug has been pulled. They saw her push a few meager forkfuls of food past her resisting mouth before abandoning the effort entirely and retreating to her room, where she spent the long evenings instead of joining them by the fire as she used to do. They saw her grow increasingly gaunt and hollow-eyed. Finally, they asked Addie if she knew what was wrong.

"Grayson Lowrey." She spat out the name. "And it's all my fault too."

"Your fault?" Eric asked.

"Not really, I don't suppose. I warned Kristin, told her that Gray was hard on women who cared. I guess I didn't make the warning strong enough."

"Is there anything we can do?" Betsy's question was asked with a soft urgency.

"For lovesickness? Not a thing, unless you can make a few months, probably a few years in this case, pass by real quick."

So those who loved Kristin were nearly as apprehensive as she was when they heard the familiar grind of the engine of the Bronco straining up the mountain. They were just finishing lunch when the mechanical sound reached them. Kristin's chair scraped back and she bolted upright.

"Addie, could you send Laurie up to my room?" Kristin asked. Bracing herself to make the request in public, she added, "And please tell Gray not to come up. I don't want to see him." It was the only way she could survive this ordeal. Even one glimpse of Gray would undo her.

"I'll take your afternoon class," Eric volunteered.

Kristin smiled wanly. Everyone had been so kind to her, treating her like a convalescent. The worst part of it was, she didn't even have the strength to allay their concerns. "Thanks, I'd really appreciate that. The new instructor should be here tomorrow, so I'll just go on ahead and leave as soon as I'm done packing."

The looks of worried compassion on the three faces across from her were more than Kristin could stand. In another minute, those infernal tears would start again. "I'm only going to be down in Taos," she chided them with a commendable show of spirt. "We can visit as often as we like, whenever you all aren't busy with the lodge and I'm not getting ready for my show. Is it a deal?"

The three tried to return her artificial show of heartiness with a similar performance of their own. Kristin heard the spatter of gravel as Gray pulled up outside. Unable to continue the charade, she turned abruptly and hurried for the stairs, with Punkin', excited by the first burst of energy she'd witnessed from Kristin in a week, romping at her heels.

Kristin dragged the suitcases out from under the bed, threw them open, and began tossing clothes into them. The feel of Gray under the same roof with her seemed to force the air from her lungs, the calm from her heart. She jerked around at the first weak tap on her door. *It's only Laurie*, she had to remind herself to slow her runaway pulse. She opened the door for the little girl.

"Punkin'," Laurie cried out, rushing past Kristin to hug the bewildered retriever. Before she could shut the door, Kristin saw Addie coming up the stairs.

"I won't keep you," the lodge manager whispered. "Gray asked me to tell you that he'd be in his office for the next couple of hours to give you plenty of time to"—Addie stumbled on the word—"to leave. He also asked me to tell you he'd like to talk with you. He'll be waiting in his office."

"He'll have a long wait, Addie. I've gone to him once too often."

Addie patted the hand that Kristin had wrapped around the doorframe, then left. Kristin turned to Laurie. The thought that this would be the last time she ever saw the little girl tore at her, surprising her with the depth of her attachment to the child.

"Hello, Laurie. How has your vacation been?"

"Pretty good. Except . . . you know what?" Laurie didn't wait for a reply. "You're a lot nicer to me than my mommy is. Aren't mommies supposed to be nice to their little girls?"

Kristin nodded.

"I'll bet you'd be nice if you had a little girl." Before Kristin could answer, Laurie barreled on ahead with more pressing matters. "Daddy took me to the zoo in Albuquerque after I came back from my mommy's house." As Laurie babbled on about her trip to the zoo, Kristin groped for a way to say good-bye.

Laurie interrupted her thoughts. "When can we go skiing again?"

She couldn't hedge what she had to say. "I doubt that we'll be skiing together again, Laurie. I'm leaving High Country. That was what I wanted to tell you." Kristin was unprepared for the way the little girl's face crumpled beneath an instantaneous onslaught of unhappiness. Kristin saw all her own feelings of rejection and sorrow mirrored in the downturned mouth, the quivering chin, the glistening eyes. A rivulet of oozing warmth opened up inside Kristin as she gathered the little girl into her arms. Tears matted Laurie's eyelashes into spiky clumps.

"Don't cry, Button." The nickname slid easily off of Kristin's tongue. "I'll come and visit you in Santa Fe." The decision was made in a second. There was no reason, and now Kristin realized, no way, that she wouldn't see Laurie again. And she didn't give a damn what Gray had to say about it.

"Really?" Laurie asked skeptically, hesitantly. "At my school?"

"Really," Kristin answered.

The tears were gone like the briefest of summer squalls that leave behind an earth freshened by their passing. Laurie beamed at the thought of Kristin coming to see her at school. "You can see where I sleep. Can Punkin' come?"

"She wouldn't miss the trip for anything," Kristin assured her.

"Cool! I can show her to Rosemary. Rosemary's my best friend. Jennifer Armijo used to be my best friend, but not anymore."

For the first time in a week, Kristin felt her old lightness of mood return as she listened to the child rattle on. In the middle of her chatty monologue, Laurie broke off and asked, "Can I take Punkin' for a walk?"

"Why don't you just take Punkin' downstairs to play in the main hall, all right?"

Laurie bobbed her head in agreement and got up to

leave, calling Punkin' to her and squealing with delight when the dog, ever ready for an outing, responded.

"Now remember," Kristin reiterated, "I'll be coming to see you at your school later on. For now, don't go outside. Understand, Laurie?"

"Understand," she said, absorbed in leading Punkin' from the room.

Kristin turned back to her packing. She wanted to be far from High Country by the time Gray emerged from his office, but she lost track of the time as she packed her bags, then carefully wrapped her prints. By the time she was done, the blue gingham room looked as spare and empty as it had the day she'd first seen it. She lugged the first of her two bags downstairs and stowed it in the back of her station wagon. On the trip back upstairs, she saw Punkin' sprawled out in her usual spot in front of the fire. Kristin assumed that Laurie had tired of playing with the dog and had gone off to find Gray.

As she was snapping the latches closed on her second bag, a knock at her door startled her. Even more startling was finding Gray on the other side. The hurt and the wanting of him combined with such force that Kristin couldn't even look into his eyes. She didn't invite him in, but she couldn't summon the force to slam the door in his face. She felt like a swimmer caught in a roiling sea who must wait for a giant wave to break and roll over her before she can swim to safety.

"You were going to leave without speaking to me?" It was a question to which Gray already knew the answer. He didn't wait for her response, but plunged on to ask, "Kristin, how can I tell you how wrong I've been? I've done nothing but think about you, about what you said to me, for the last week."

Kristin squeezed the door shut, not wanting to hear his words, not again.

"Please," he implored, using a single hand to easily halt the door's closing, "come to my office. I don't want to talk about this in front of Laurie."

A distant alarm sounded in Kristin's head. It took her a few seconds before its significance hit her. "Laurie's not here," she said, swinging the door open. "I thought she was with you."

Gray burst into the room, his head jerking from side to side as he conducted a frenzied search of the bare room. "Where did she go?"

"Downstairs. With Punkin'. She wanted to go for a walk. I told her she couldn't go outside." Kristin telegraphed her answer.

Gray tore down the stairs, Kristin behind him. "Addie," he bellowed, "Addie." The manager came running from the kitchen, drying her hands on a dish towel.

"Heavenly days, what's all the ruckus for?"

"Have you seen Laurie?" Gray asked.

"Why, yes, she's in by the fire playing with Punkin'.

Isn't she?" A quick look told Addie that the child wasn't there. "That's where she was before I went into the kitchen to show the new cook how I mix my pie dough."

"How long ago was that?"

"Couldn't have been more than half an hour."

"Half an hour," Gray moaned.

"She's probably somewhere around the house," Kristin suggested.

Gray struggled to calm himself. He glanced around the hall, his gaze stopping at a pair of small mittens tossed onto the couch.

"Her jacket's gone."

With those three words a pillar of panic wedged itself under Kristin's backbone. Gray's face was ashen. Kristin knew that anything she was feeling was only a fraction of what Gray was undergoing. He turned and began asking every guest, every employee, if anyone had seen a little girl in a pink parka. Finally Gray heard the words he was dreading.

"Yeah," a teenaged boy answered, "I saw her go outside about half an hour ago." He gave an adolescent shrug as if to ask what the big deal was.

The gesture wasn't lost on Gray. "She has a heart problem," Gray blurted out to the astonished youth. "She's special. She can't wander off by herself. She won't know how to come back." His voice snagged with a ragged catch on the last words.

"How was I supposed to know?" the bewildered boy asked.

Gray shook his head and reached a weary hand out to touch his shoulder. "You weren't," he apologized. "I'm sorry. Come on everybody," he called out to the alerted guests and staff. "Let's start searching."

Kristin whistled for Punkin' and the dog was at her side in an instant. She grabbed one of Laurie's mittens from the couch and held it in front of the dog's nose. Punkin' had never done any hunting or tracking, but Kristin prayed she would instinctively understand what her mission was. The retriever trotted eagerly to the door as Kristin shrugged on her parka and followed, and Gray and Eric organized the other searchers.

Punkin' led off like a greyhound coming out of the starting gate at the track. Kristin was elated when Punkin' slowed down and put her coal-black nose in the snow to sniff, then set off again. Kristin's optimism waned a bit, however, when the dog began zigzagging around the lodge in a crazy circuit that led from the lesson pasture back to the front door. It plummeted completely when Punkin' started scratching on the door and whining to go back inside. The main hall of the lodge was empty. There was no sign of any searchers or of Laurie. Kristin quickly let Punkin' in, then turned back to the frozen landscape outside.

An increasing sense of urgency beat through Kristin

as she saw how long the shadows on the snow had grown in the time she'd been chasing after Punkin'. In the high mountains sunset came with a terrifying swiftness, and with it a cold that only the heartiest could withstand given the best of preparations. Laurie was neither hearty nor prepared. Kristin buckled on her skis. A dozen trails opened up around her. She knew that most of them twined along high ridges where even the slightest tumble would send the unwary sliding off into deep ravines or toward icy streams. Kristin could only imagine the choking fear that must be gripping Gray.

She dug her poles in and pushed off, following the spur of a back trail far into the dense overgrowth of pines. She screamed Laurie's name until her throat was raw, listening after each yell for any hint of a response. All she heard were the echoes of other searchers shouting the same name. She skied on. There was no chance of finding small footprints to follow. The trails were all so packed down by constant skiing that Laurie's fragile weight would never have left a dent in the icy surface. After a few more minutes, Kristin stopped. She'd gone too far. It wasn't possible that Laurie, on foot, could have covered as much ground as she had on skis. She headed back, but veered off the trail on her return trip to peer down gullies and into culverts. Her search spiraled out into a larger circle as she remembered more potential traps hidden throughout the forest she knew so well.

As the sun dipped ever lower, the cold began biting into Kristin with an increasingly fierce sting. However, every time that she considered heading for the warmth of the lodge, she would think of Laurie, alone and confused and far colder than she was, and she would drive herself on to yet another possible spot. The sun's rays were slicing into her eyes now, a farewell burst of brilliance that would come to an end with a fearsome swiftness as night fell. Kristin knew then that she had no time left. If she didn't head back immediately, the search party would think that it had another missing person on its hands.

As the horizon slivered off ever larger sections of the sun, Kristin became fully aware of just how far she had wandered, of how far off the trail she was. There was still light enough left for her to make it back, she reckoned, but she'd have to hurry. Goading herself on, she began skiing a bit faster than was safe in the fading light, a bit too fast to react when her ski slipped under a loop of root hidden by a snowdrift. Her arms windmilling frantically for the balance she'd lost, Kristin tumbled headfirst into the snow. Her ski, however, was anchored fast by the hidden noose. Even as she fell, Kristin felt the tearing pain that shot through her as her ankle was wrenched by the spill.

Snow found its way up her sleeves, down her neck, into her nose, and under her parka. Kristin brushed off as much as she could, hearing her father's voice warning his scouts that "to stay dry in the mountains is to survive." She felt an icy trickle worming its way down her back where the snow had broken through her defenses, and she knew that it was more vital than ever now that she get indoors. Her head throbbing, she tried to stand. The pain that lanced through her leg left her gasping and clinging to her poles like a cripple to his crutches. Though she refused to let herself consciously think the thought, deep within her Kristin knew that, if she allowed herself to fall back to the snow, there was a good chance she'd never get up again. A wave of nauseating dizziness rolled over her, leaving her field of vision speckled with a swarm of whirling black dots.

She forced herself to breathe deeply. *Don't pass out. Don't pass out.* She beat the words through her brain like a chant to a cruel god, a god who would kill on the slightest whim. And still the sun slid lower.

"Hello." Kristin's call was devoured by the great trees and deep snow. The enormity of both suddenly struck her, bringing with it the full awareness of her own frailty. The possibility that she might not make it back to the lodge opened within her. It started as a hairline crack that an earthquake of panic wedged open until it was a bottomless abyss.

"Help!" Her next cry held fear. "Help, someone, help me!" She heard her screams and recognized the seeds of hysteria in them.

Calm down. The order was stern, stern as any her father had ever issued. For the first time in a week, she allowed herself the thoughts she had fought so hard against, thoughts of Gray. The memories of their night together, of his hands, his lips on her, diverted her, stemming the tide of panic that threatened to engulf her reason.

Kristin slid forward on her good leg; then, leaning her weight on her poles, she brought up her injured leg. A ragged bolt of pain shuddered through her. She bit her lip to stanch the flow of the tears trying to sneak out from beneath her eyelids. She had to make it to the trail before the last glimmerings of daylight were lost. She slid forward on her good leg. Then the injured one. She sucked in a steadying breath and did it again. And again. As the pain beat through her, Kristin fought it down by telling herself that each step brought her that much closer to Gray. She knew she was tricking herself, but the comforting lie gave her strength.

The first time she heard her name called out in that booming, male voice that her heart knew better than its own beat, Kristin thought the trick had been carried too far, that she had begun to hear lies now in other voices. The second time her name was shouted, her whole being rose up to return the call. Then she sank down into the snow.

"Kristin—God, are you all right?" Gray crashed through the low barrier of brush that separated them, bursting through it with enough force to splinter a solid barricade.

"It hurts, Gray," she whimpered, clasping her ankle, unable to keep up her courage a moment longer.

Gray removed both their pairs of skis and planted them in the snow. Tenderly, he pulled down Kristin's sock. The skin was stretched tight over the hot, swollen mass of her ankle.

"We've got to get you back to the lodge." Gray slid an arm under Kristin's knees and another under her arms and hoisted her off the snow. Kristin wrapped her arms around Gray's neck and laid her head against his chest. The jostling made her ankle ache, but she barely noticed. Abruptly, she jerked her head up.

"Laurie?" she started to ask, but Gray hushed her.

"Don't worry," he said, his voice a comforting rumble against Kristin's ear, "she's tucked in a warm bed. Punkin' found her."

"Punkin'? But she was at the lodge."

"Precisely where Laurie was. Punkin' kept whining and whimpering until someone followed her to the basement door. Laurie was down there, asleep on top of a pile of old blankets. Seems she'd gone outside, then come back in to look for the sled I'd bought her for Christmas and stored down in the basement. When she couldn't reach it, she stopped for a little nap."

Kristin sagged with relief against the wall of Gray's

chest, further soothed by the rocking of the long strides that took them closer to the lodge.

"Now that I've got you trapped," Gray began, "you're going to have to listen to what I've got to say to you."

"Please don't, Gray." Kristin made the request as forcefully as she could. "Just let me go on with my life as best I'm able."

"I can't let you go on with any life that doesn't include me. You were right, Kristin. I've used Laurie as a shield against life for too long. I didn't even realize what I was doing until last week. You made me see. You and Harrell. I saw him not too long after you left, and I couldn't even begin to hide how torn up I was. We talked. With his help, his insight, I was able to face something I'd hidden from since the moment I first saw Laurie. Much as I loved her, I doubted that anyone else could. Not really. My guilt at feeling like my own child was basically unlovable drove me to an overprotectiveness that excluded anyone either Laurie or I might care about or become attached to the way we were attached to Jan."

Gray spoke with an effort. Kristin couldn't tell if it came from carrying her or from the difficulty of what he had to say.

"I couldn't believe that you could truly care for Laurie. If I had any doubts, though, they were erased today. Kristin, I've been a wrongheaded fool. Please, don't let it be too late. I know I've hurt you. I want to spend the rest of our lives together making it up to you. Kristin, I love you."

Kristin looked away in time to see the sun's final curve impaled on the spiky top of Diablo Peak. She remembered the joy and heartache she'd discovered there, a discovery that was repeated again in Gray's bed at Powderhorn. "Gray, you hurt me terribly I don't think I could survive if it happened again. My heart's not strong enough."

"Kristin, love, it doesn't have to be. There'll be no more hurting between us. Ever. You're too precious to me. Kristin, I've hurt too. I've ached from wanting you, all of you. Your laugh, your kiss, your vibrance, the life you've brought to my life. You have an equal power to cause me pain, you know."

They walked in silence broken only by the sound of Gray's breathing, of the beat of his heart, of his footsteps crunching over the icy trail. As Kristin looked to the far peak, almost as if she thought she might find an answer written there upon its craggy slopes, a magical veil was passed over it, cloaking the mountain in hazy pink. She looked at Gray to find his rugged features shimmering with the same pastel radiance. It was all around them, deepening as the seconds passed to a darker rose that licked the frosty snows with a warm blaze of color.

"Alpenglow," Gray said. Even as Gray spoke, the tinted luminescence began to fade, giving way to the coming darkness. "I wish I could have made it last longer." Gray's wish was a saddened acceptance of what had slipped, at last and irrevocably, beyond his control.

Kristin was grateful for that resignation. She couldn't bear taking the risk of finding out that Gray's burst of love would be as short-lived as the alpenglow.

Gray's lengthy strides took them ever closer to the lodge, to the moment when their paths would part forever. Kristin would not stop him. Not this time. But the choice was not hers.

The rocking stopped and Gray stood stock still in the dimming light. "Damn it, woman," he burst out. "We're not some natural phenomenon doomed to fizzle out after a few glorious moments. We're two people who love each other. It was you who showed me that I can't shield myself from love any more than I can, or even should, shelter Laurie from it. Kristin, please, don't leave me. Stay with me. Here in the mountains. Be my wife." Gray's proposal was tinged with a note of sadness. He knew it would be refused. Kristin's silence confirmed his gloomy certainty.

Kristin felt the despairing sigh that sank Gray's chest. She looked into his face, and the love she felt for the good, strong, misguided man who held her in his arms rose up within her in a dizzying wave. It forced her to realize that, no matter what the risks, together, she and Gray had to *make* his words come true. Alpenglow *was* a heavenly gift, given for only a few precious seconds, just as life, just as love was. Neither one could be hoarded or protected, preserved under a bell jar and kept from harm.

Kristin's kiss was brief, as short as the squall of an infant that starts a new life, as short as the shimmering radiance of the alpenglow. But Gray returned it in a gentle, cherishing way that sealed the pledge they both made to a future together.

"Kristin." He uttered her name with a muffled wonderment, then began walking again, hurrying now to bring his love into the warmth and light.